THE
GARDEN
LADY

SUSAN DWORKIN

Divided Light Projects, LLC

In loving memory of my sister,
Ruth Levine Reuben

part

1

ONE.

The Former Maxie Dash

Maxine Vandeblinken sucked on a chunk of lemon, then chewed a cube of ice and continued automatically, lemon, ice, lemon, ice, lemon, ice, more lemon. She was having an attack of aggravation, caused by an email. *We'll never make a fall opening, Mrs. Vandeblinken. The weather has just been too crazy. The plans are just too complex. We'll be lucky if we can open a year from next spring.*

Of course, the email was not unexpected. But still it descended like a curtain on her big plans. Maxine had looked forward to opening the Frank Bass Memorial Garden, a monument to the work of her first husband. There were supposed to be banquets and press receptions and guided tours. However, for months now, heavy downpours had been bludgeoning the rich New Jersey town of Schraalenberg where Maxine lived. The storm sewers spewed excess. The lawns brimmed. Construction of the dredged and re-routed stream bed, the romantic stone walking bridge, and the pathways for the blind had not even begun. Her fabulous Garden lay dormant in a puddle of mud.

Maxine hated that. False starts. Returned tickets. You were all psyched and ready to rock and roll, and boom, they called the show.

Now, at ten o'clock on a Saturday morning in May, yet another storm poured down. Black clouds formed such a dense cover over Schraalenberg that the light of day could barely penetrate. Robins did not know whether to sing.

Crunching ice with her back teeth, Maxine snatched the plastic-covered newspaper from her front steps and spread it out on the black granite kitchen counter. She read the headlines, then, scowling, tried the television. A trim meteorologist announced that the rain would be "torrential at times." Everybody who could possibly stay off the road was advised to do so.

Maxine took a ragged, anxious breath. Her husband Albert was flying today. He had called to say he would soon finish his work in Verona and leave for Milan and then Zurich and from there, he would fly home.

She hated the thought of Albert in turbulence.

The previous evening, Maxine had gone out on the town with her friend, Ceecee Blochner. The two ladies were picked up and delivered, from every door to every door, by a handsome driver in a navy Mercedes, which Maxine had hired for the night. The slow ride through the wet city streets afforded them views of the homeless lying on beds of rags, sheltered by doorways, by cartons that had originally delivered refrigerators.

"Do you ever forget?" Ceecee asked. "Do you ever forget how hungry we were?"

"Not for one minute," Maxine said.

They drove past the place that had once been a nightspot where they had spent some wonderful evenings with men who adored them.

"Show me your pictures of Gladdy's baby," Maxine said. "I know you have them."

Ceecee offered pictures of her newest grandchild, a jolly, black-haired girl with sparkling eyes. Maxine held the pictures close, as though the luscious smell of the baby might be inhaled from them, and she sighed with longing.

The dinner, at a smart Italian place in the west 40s, was over-priced, its much-praised rigatoni cooked so *al dente* that one of Maxine's fillings fell out in it. The play – a celebrated hit; rave reviews – was just awful.

Emerging from the ladies' room, Ceecee looked old and tired to Maxine. Her elegant suit hung crookedly. Her long hair in its Evita chignon was dyed too black. Her strong craftswoman fingers seemed skinny and breakable.

"You know, I was thinking," Ceecee said, "I was thinking that now, with my Herman gone and the girls running the business in Tucson, maybe I might give up the Rodriguez Fancy office in New York, retire, go back to the desert, you know, where I could just be a gray grandma and nobody would give a damn if I put on a little weight."

"Great idea," Maxine said.

"Maybe someday you could come too, and we could live together again, like two old sisters."

"But for that, Albert Vandeblinken would have to die," Maxine said. "And I don't think he could possibly take so much time away from his business."

Ceecee fell asleep in the hired car. Her head lolled. She snored. When they pulled up at her building, Maxine walked her past the doorman, rode with her up to the apartment, greeted her little dog, Crispy, helped her undress, got her into bed and tucked her in.

Once or twice during the long ride home to New Jersey, Maxine caught the driver looking at her in the rear-view mirror. Despite the lessons of the evening – *we're over the hill; we've lost it; we're finished* – her heart quickened. She could feel a fan coming on. Wonderful feeling.

"Mrs. Vandeblinken...excuse me for asking...but weren't you on television...back in the 70s...?"

"Yes."

"I knew it! I knew it was you! I loved those cigarette ads you did – *'Inhale, baby, and get a taste of me...'*" he sang, a pretty good imitation. "You were one of the reasons I decided to be an actor."

"Really! I had no idea those commercials poisoned the mind as well as the body."

The driver grinned. His eyes sought hers in the mirror.

"Well, you were great in all those shows, you should know that. When you played the secretary to the mob boss and the next-door neighbor who was hot for the exterminator, and oh yeah, in that soap commercial with the baby and the gold bubbles, boy oh boy, you were just so… I had a real crush on you."

At her front door, Maxine did not wait for him to come around and hand her out of the car. She got out quickly by herself and entered her house, flipped on the rotunda lights and then, at the very last minute, knowing how attractively the lights glowed behind her, she turned, and in the low, sonorous, once somewhat familiar voice of Maxie Dash, professional beauty, supporting soap player, spokesperson for discontinued products, she said: "Thank you for your kind thoughts, young man. Give me your business card. When next I need a navy Mercedes, I'll be sure to call you."

THE NEXT DAY, PRECISELY at the moment when Maxine heard that the rain would be torrential and began worrying about her husband Albert in turbulence, a baby blue Brights International Express van, called a "BIXvan" by its television commercials, pulled out of the Newark headquarters lot and turned north on the Turnpike toward Schraalenberg.

Alongside the van came a convoy of refuse trucks heading for the landfill that was known locally as Garbage Mountain. They clattered and clamored, sounding loose and rickety, seeding the BIX driver's mind with fear that one of them might suddenly crumble and dump its stinking load on spotless passing vehicles like his.

You couldn't see Garbage Mountain on this dark morning, but the squawks of the trash gulls told you it was out there, an open grave, always waiting for more. People actually lived near it. Right under its looming shadow. The young BIX driver didn't know how anyone could bear to do that.

Eventually the trucks dipped off onto a shrouded exit and disappeared from view. The driver was happy to see them go. He felt grateful to be light and sprightly, brightly colored and sparsely loaded with special Saturday packages. As he entered the boulevards of Schraalenberg, he plowed right into the puddles, Gene Kelly-style, just for the fun of the splash. Lightning flashed. The van lit up like Hollywood and went toodling toward its destination: Fifteen Willow Cascade.

The BIXvan driver found it not by seeing the number but by spotting the willows. He saw an elaborate gate, made of the address wrought in iron script, flanked by two enormous lanterns that he did not know were relics of a Borgia palace. From the gate, undulating willows cascaded over a mile-long driveway that ended at a very big house.

He pressed the call button, backed up and turned the van around, plainly displaying the BIX insignia for the scarlet security eye. Then he called the number on the package.

"Mrs. Vandeblinken? This is Brights International Express. I'm right outside your door with a special urgent Saturday delivery. Just look through your TV guard box, you'll see me."

"I'm not expecting anything," said the woman within.

"It's an envelope, ma'am. Marked 'Documents.' Return address: Monaco Ville. The sender is Herr Albert Vandeblinken."

"Well then my husband couldn't have sent it because he never calls himself Herr, and anyway, he wasn't supposed to be in Monaco, and besides, Albert himself is arriving later this morning so why would he not bring the envelope in his own hand?"

"I couldn't say, ma'am."

Maxine didn't really want to let the BIX man approach her house. It wasn't that she felt afraid of him. Everybody knew you could trust that famous baby blue uniform. However, she had decided to fight off her Garden postponement blues by washing the dog. Counting on perfect solitude, with her housekeeper and gardeners off for the day, she had just sudsed up her young russet retriever, Hannibal, for a nice shampoo. She was wearing her comfy pajamas and no makeup. And Maxine never let anyone see her without her makeup.

She sighed and buzzed the driver through the gate. While he negotiated the driveway, she whipped her long hair into a knot, changed into a pink silk caftan, put on lipstick, powder, blush, eyeliner and earrings, and was ready with a pleasant smile at her front door. He handed her the baby blue envelope. She signed his computer. Before she closed the door, she began opening the envelope. The driver was climbing into his van when he heard her scream.

She screamed and screamed.

The young man ran back to Maxine. She had fallen to her knees. Her alarmed dog raced to assist her, spraying soap suds all over the BIX envelope that had come from Monaco. Its contents spilled.

Two photographs. Different angles. A white-bearded man. Naked. Sprawled on his back. Smashed glasses on his neck. Between his thick, bristly, pepper and salt eyebrows, a black hole where a bullet had entered. Underneath his head, a long spill of blood. A severed hand lay on his chest, a woman's hand, with painted fingernails and many rings. Gore dripped over the man's torso.

TWO.

Brights' Lunacy

Sam EUPHEMIA WAS JOGGING BY the Pacific just before sunset. Best time, he thought. The great orange ball took over. Gorgeousness set in, sculpting the clouds, glittering the sea, a sight so distracting that it was easy to stop thinking and vacate the tensions of the business week. Let the Verdi in the headset overwhelm the mind. Let the legs and lungs do all the work.

Streams of sweat swept through Sam's hair, pooled on the ridge of his dark, low slung brows and wet down his Teddy Roosevelt moustache. He was running fast, running like a kid again. He was actually smiling when he returned to his office for a shower and a night of work. Then New York called to say somebody had murdered Albert Vandeblinken.

"Goddammit," Sam muttered. He tore off his T-shirt and wiped his face with it and kicked a waste basket across the room. It wasn't that he felt bad about Albert's death. It was that he knew that his boss, Jim Brights, the President and founder of Brights International Express, was going to be deeply disappointed by this news, because Jim had always wanted to be the one who brought down Vandeblinken and now somebody else had beaten him to it. Sympathy for Jim and his screwed vendetta flooded Sam's heart.

From the time a dozen years earlier when Sam had come to work for BIX in California, Jim Brights had engaged him in the pursuit of some dark truth about Vandeblinken. Jim believed that the elegant

Swiss, an aircraft broker, had at one time trafficked in planes with falsified crash histories and bogus parts, had them beautified, looking good as new, and sent them aloft with innocents aboard. But he had no actual proof; only promising leads; suspicious connections; only an obsession. Brights' Lunacy, Sam called it. The peculiar madness of an otherwise supremely level-headed leader.

Just speaking of Vandeblinken made Jim angry. The maze of wrinkles crisscrossing his face throbbed from the rush of blood. His hands clenched spasmodically. Sam had once seen him snap a pencil unawares.

This unrelenting antipathy stemmed from an incident that had occurred in the 50s, when Jim's air courier business was just getting started. He had heard tell about four small, reconditioned British transports available for a very good price. He went to see the planes where they were parked in a hangar on a Sicilian hillside. A Dutch friend, an aircraft designer, potential partner in Jim's nascent venture, came along.

The Dutchman had been taken to Germany as a prisoner during the war and forced to work in an aircraft factory, which had burned itself to the ground rather than be captured by the advancing Russians. He vividly recalled how the parts and pieces had flown out of the place before the end, to wind up in which aircraft no one knew. Examining the transports, the Dutchman shook his head, smelling uninspected components, unreported accidents, cosmetic repairs. So Jim Brights did not buy the planes.

He later heard that they were bought by a Swiss pilot named Vandeblinken, who spruced them up and sold them back into operation. When the first one disintegrated in midair, Jim notified the European air safety authorities, detailing his fears that the other three would meet similar fates and pleading that they be tracked down and taken out of service. He was not an important man then, and attention was not paid. When the second and third crashed, one in Italy, one in Scotland, they had already been bought and sold several times since Vandeblinken had acquired them. He could no longer be held in any way responsible.

The fourth was never found.

"I kept imagining," Jim said, "kept imagining that fourth plane disassembled, with all its parts bought for cheap and installed in dozens of aircraft. Every time I heard the stories about old used parts showing up in planes that had promised to be all brand new, I thought of Vandeblinken. If a man could do it once, he might have done it again. Might have made a profitable habit of it over the years."

He assigned Sam, then his newest and most promising young executive, to writing periodic reports to flesh out his suspicions. "This is what you're going to look for," he said. "You're going to look for unexplained crashes of little aircraft, most likely in continental Europe, where there was no evidence of pilot error or bad weather or a pre-existing structural defect or metal fatigue, and the cause goes on the books as a mystery. Then look for Vandeblinken in the background."

Eager to excel in his new job, Sam called every connection he could muster – French cops, Swiss freight forwarders, old Army buddies now working in private transport. His reports were heavy with first-hand information, but they could establish nothing.

"Here are some cases where used or bogus parts are suspected," he wrote. "Italy, 1980. Belgian honeymooners in a charter crash in the Adriatic. No survivors. Switzerland, 1983. A USAF colonel takes his grandson flying over the Alps in a rental. They hit a power line when they go down. Albania, 1989. A private jet plows into a hillside. The six passengers are well known drug smugglers. The cops don't follow up because they are so happy these guys are dead. In all cases, junk parts are suspected.

"Albert Vandeblinken and his son Marcus cannot be found anywhere in all this. Not selling, not reselling, not refurbishing, not buying, not leasing, nothing. If they ever purveyed bad equipment, they did it long ago and got away with it and now they are *M. Clean et Fils, Ltd.*

"I'm really sorry, Jim."

The report was filed. So were the half dozen others that followed. Then the report writing passed on to lower ranks as Sam, doggedly growing his career at BIX, rose to become Director of Strategic Operations for the Western Hemisphere. He no longer really believed in Brights' Lunacy, which seemed to him an apparition, a hunch which had gone nowhere. But he kept his eye on the mystery crashes and stayed in touch with the developing problem of bogus parts, cheaply manufactured knock-offs, way below standard quality, which were showing up on black markets in Europe and Miami.

A fucking sieve, Miami, said the inspector from the FAA, speaking mainly but not only of drugs.

Meanwhile, Albert Vandeblinken matured into one of the aviation elite, selling private jets to the wealthy, commuting between his office in Newark and the Zurich headquarters run by his son, living quietly with his glamorous wife in a palace in New Jersey. The only time his name appeared in the papers was when the son was killed, apparently in some drug-related violence. Sam knew plenty of people in the courier business who had visited the grieving father's home to pay condolences. Albert was well-liked. Respected. Established and enormously success-ful. Nothing to report. And still Jim Brights scowled and reddened and clenched.

A BIG GUY, SAM EUPHEMIA had played tight end on his high school football team and still carried his size like power. He used silence skill-fully, to confound and confuse and intimidate. He tended to get right to the point. Hardly ever asked "How're you doing?" or made small talk. He dressed very well. Wore custom made shirts with French cuffs and gold cufflinks that glared. He never spoke about his roots or his home town. Jim Brights was known to be his mentor, at once paternal and brotherly, a professor of strategies. A business magazine characterized Sam as "laconic, family-less, hard to know, competent in more languages than he lets on, and fiercely loyal to his boss."

Pacing his office, still sweaty from the jog, Sam turned on all his media and contacted his sources. The lurid details of Albert's death had leaked quickly. Most of the industry gossip assumed that Vandeblinken had been done in by a jealous lover or husband, who had as an extra measure of revenge lopped off his cheating woman's left hand. A New Jersey detective named Bobby Meeker, known to Sam because of a pornography smuggling bust, suspected Maxine.

"We got a really well-connected woman here," Meeker explained. "Famous fashion plate. Dated lotsa big shots. Major investor in a company that makes high end boots for ladies. Big donor to all kindsa causes, from the Navajo Scholarship Fund to the Opera. Her first husband was a photographer. Took pictures of her naked and would you believe they ended up in *museums*. A woman like this might think she's hot shit, know what I mean, Sam? Might feel like she doesn't have to put up with humiliation. Might get really pissed and hire some bad guys." In New Jersey, Detective Meeker hitched his pants. Sam could hear the jingle of the change in his pocket. "And then, we gotta consider Albert's dough."

However, Sam Euphemia was considering something far worse.

He stood like a pillar at his office window, consulting the dark western skies, listening to the rattle of the overseeing copters, tapping one fist against his moustache. He was remembering those old reports he had written for his boss. He pictured the Air Force colonel and his grandson on fire, sparks cascading onto the snow. He saw the honeymooners in pieces, floating; the gangsters strewn over the hillside with their wreckage.

Two years ago, Marcus Vandeblinken had been murdered. Now Albert was dead by a savage hand. Surely there must be a connection. Maybe the people who had killed Marcus and Albert had nothing to do with drugs or sex or money. Maybe like Jim Brights, they were fixated on mysterious plane crashes. Maybe someone or something they valued had gone down, and they were engaged in vengeance, seeking justice, and like Jim Brights, had reason to believe that the Vandeblinkens were masterminds of a murderous criminal operation and deserved to die. And if that were true, then there could be additional planes with compromised equipment still flying, deadly pretenders that might slip undetected into a fleet of aircraft employed by a big package delivery company that was famous for being absolutely safe.

part

———

2

THREE.

One Last Man

IN THE YEARS BETWEEN HER marriages, Maxine did indeed enjoy long liaisons with several men who satisfied her expensive tastes and treated her well and left her with an accumulation of valuable goods. These affairs ended amicably. They were open; public; mentioned in certain show business biographies. But there were other men too – secret one-night stands, casual flings, passing fancies, no-name monsters.

They never appeared in any dossier prepared by Detective Meeker. But they left their mark. Several just smacked Maxine around, blackening her eyes. Another knocked out two of her teeth and put a hairline crack in her jaw. Another broke her wrist.

Maxine took to recovering from such episodes at Ceecee's house, where Ceecee's husband, Herman Blochner, lectured her wearily and Ceecee just ranted, hiding Maxine from her daughters as best she could, and when she couldn't, inventing fantastic explanations for her injuries. The girls never believed her. Her tough daughter, Gladdy, said: "You know of course, Mom, that Aunt Maxie is totally nuts."

Maxine lived on the pills her shrink had given her. She visited him sometimes three and four times a week in an effort to understand why she deliberately sought out these agents as weapons against her loveliness, to ruin the very thing which had brought her wealth and success. She pictured her perfect exterior and her anguished spirit rolling and shrieking and tearing at each other in a wild catfight that could only end in her destruction. For a while, she *became* the struggle. A potential suicide. Textbook case for those few healers who specialized in the distorted world of the very pretty.

She worked steadily all through this nightmare time. Made her dates for the television ads. Flew to Los Angeles for her supporting roles, which she learned in a flash on the plane. Produced believable alibis for her many friends. Only Ceecee and her family knew the truth, and they never told. And the time passed. And a new time came.

One day in her 49th year, she stood naked in her bathroom, surrounded by mirrors, and she noticed, behind one knee, a blue vein.

In that instant, the war between Maxine's spirit and her flesh ended. The flesh had lost. The abusers disappeared from her life. Like other women who really don't want to grow old alone, she started looking concertedly for one last man.

THEY WERE INTRODUCED AT THE opening of a new musical. Albert was an investor, part of a European financial coalition that had backed the show. Maxine had just returned from Los Angeles, where she had taped an episode of a hit series in which she played someone's visiting mother-in-law. Her date for the opening of the musical, a respected jurist, one-time-lover-become-friend, wanted her to marry him now that his wife was dead. His hands trembled. He needed her help to settle into his seat.

Amid the babble of introductions in the lobby before the show, with all those savvy New York businessmen surrounding her, admiring her beauty, chatting her up with their durable jokes, the elegant guy from Switzerland snagged her attention somehow. Maybe it was the surprisingly low voice. The complex hazel eyes. The fascinating contrast between the trim white beard on his face and the black hair on his wrist that slipped into view when he reached out to take her hand and touch it to his lips.

From her seat, right before the house lights went down, Maxine turned to get another look at Albert Vandeblinken.

He grinned at her.

Dimples.

She made inquiries. He was an aircraft broker, in business with his son. Offices in Zurich and Verona. Expanding into America. Divorced. Living temporarily at the Pierre and looking for an apartment on the East Side, or possibly a house in the suburbs.

He called her a week later and took her to dinner at Lutèce. They asked each other questions, divulged very little, and found to their relief that they knew no one in common. The week after that, he asked her to accompany him to a dinner party in Westchester. Most of the men present were in the shipping business.

"I was once in a play about shipping," Maxine said. "It had lots of fog. I played a good hearted whore."

The wives of the dinner party, terminally bored by maritime stories, perked up like watered daisies and begged her to continue. Soon she had them all laughing at O'Neill's romantic play and fog machines run amuck and even shipping. She could feel Albert's pleasure in her performance. It heated her arms and her face.

Albert often took Maxine into large, voluble crowds of people, a different crowd each time. He seemed to want to get to know everyone in New York, and although he himself was a rather quiet man, he sought the company of storytellers. Since reports of his wealth preceded him, Maxine would see him being hit on at parties by ambitious young women in the prime of their beauty. He was always friendly and nice to them. But he clearly preferred Maxine.

"He's got taste," Ceecee explained in her renowned know-it-all manner. "Doesn't want some chippie on his arm, making him look used and ridiculous."

Albert had a calm about him that relaxed Maxine. He always wore the softest clothing, silks and cashmeres. His shoes were custom made of leather so pliable that they might as well have been slippers. They made no sound. You never heard him enter the room.

After a long business trip to Europe during which he had not called her even once, Albert drove Maxine out to a private airport and showed her a plane. She felt a little annoyed, first because he had not called her in so long, second because she was wearing her silver silk brocade, which had no business dragging along the floor of some fucking hangar, and third because she was hungry. To make up for a slowing metabolism, she had taken to eating one small meal a day, and she had not eaten it yet.

Three deferential guys in white work coveralls stood around the plane while Albert inspected it. Their respect for him impressed her. The narrowing of his eyes as he circled the gleaming machine, the way his taut, tennis player's body came to attention, the way he touched one finger to the fuselage and held it there, like a medium seeking a message from the other side, all this fascinated and attracted her.

"Shall I buy this plane for you, Maxine?" he asked.

"I'd rather have dinner," she said.

Apparently, it was just the sort of answer he wanted. He kissed her, his eyelashes tickling. They saw each other steadily after that. It was a passionate relationship but not a lot of laughs.

Maxine was still fabulously beautiful. The surgery she had undergone to lift her breasts and her eyelids and smooth her chin was minor, "a mere tweaking", one doctor had said, because she was in such good shape to begin with. But three blue veins now popped behind her knee. She knew time had her number. When they started casting you as a visiting senior, and your old friends had the trembles, and you were down to one meal a day, you could have no doubt about that.

She was concerned about the future. She wanted to feel sure that she could live out her days in peace and comfort, with enough left over to take care of those for whom she felt responsible. She already had a million dollars of her own, accumulated during a lifetime of continual labor. However, she feared it might not be enough, that a war or a depression, a thieving broker or even just a great wind would come and blow it away, and she and Ceecee would be hungry again, and she wanted more. She had three fur coats in her closet. She would have preferred four. (In particular, she had a hankering for a floor length silver fox cape, although it might take some nerve to wear such a thing these days.) Yes,

Frank Dash had left her a beautiful apartment in Manhattan, but she wanted a house too, with acreage. She wanted jewels in her safe deposit box and art in her living room, great art, hard stuff that she could sell in a pinch. And truthfully, she was feeling a little tired. She wanted a final relationship, a regular marriage, something simple, restful, dependable. That's what she wanted.

So when Albert Vandeblinken asked her to ride out to New Jersey with him, to see the estate which he had just purchased and into which he had already moved some of his possessions, Maxine felt excited. "This could work," she said to Ceecee. "This could be the ticket."

FOUR.
In the Vault

It WAS SPRINGTIME. MAXINE DRESSED very carefully in a gauzy, rose-colored frock and a wide-brimmed hat with vermilion flowers on it. Albert walked her over the grounds and through the empty rooms. She knew she was being tested and that if she passed the test, she could be the lady of this luxurious house. She summoned all her camera-trained close-up skills to veil her true feelings, exhibiting enough admiration to flatter Albert but not so much as to seem, God forbid, eager.

This exercise in self-control got a lot harder when Albert took her into his vault.

The vault could only be accessed through the refrigerator.

First you removed the contents of the top shelf. Milk juice whatever. Then you removed the shelf itself. Then you passed a certain card into a certain slot and closed the refrigerator and it quietly pivoted and slid aside, like a polite doorman. "*Et voilà!*" said Maxine. "Albert's vault."

Ceecee rolled her eyes. "You would say anything to make me laugh."

"That is true," Maxine said. "But the refrigerator thing is true also."

She did not tell Ceecee what she had seen in the vault, the works of art, the money, the jewels. She never mentioned the mobile sculpture created by the great Alexander Calder that hung suspended from the ceiling and turned slowly around and around, in a perpetual motion of response to the slightest breath. How could she force her friend to know what she herself was always trying to put out of her own mind?

"I should like us to be married, Maxine," Albert said in the vault. "We shall live in this house. I hope that is all right with you."

She laughed and took his hand and held it to her breast, trying not to see the stacks of cash piled in a pair of cut crystal bowls, each bowl perched on the back of a carved terracotta elephant. She kissed him, biting his bottom lip to anchor herself to his mouth. However, Albert would not be anchored. He held her away from him, for he had more to say. She was forced to notice a bronze statue of a cowboy on horseback, his hat and his moustache blown back, his horse snorting, with legs curled under in a gallop, and around the neck of the horse, five long strands of natural pearls. Maxine reached for Albert's shirt.

"No," he said. "Listen to me. Pay attention." Some of the pearls were pink. Some were black. Some gray. Diamond clasp. "Whenever we go out to an event which is important to me, I will select one or two of these jewels for you to wear." At the corner of her eye, she saw a white marble swan, wild wings outstretched, about to ravish a naked nymph. The nymph wore heavy gold bangle bracelets on each wrist, and the swan bore on one rigid wing a pair of ruby drop earrings cloaked in diamonds. "Maxine, are you listening?"

"Fine, fine, stop being such a businessman. Kiss me," she insisted, reaching for his belt, slipping her hand inside his trousers. He grabbed her hand and held it very tightly, hurting her.

"You must never come in here on your own," he said. "Never. Am I clear? If you do, I will understand that you have gone through my things in order to find the card that unlocks the vault. And I shall feel unable to trust you. A man has to be able to trust his wife."

"A woman ought to be able to live with the man she loves without fear," Maxine whispered, nibbling at his neck.

"I want you to fear me, Maxie."

"Oh Albert…" she laughed, "You are sometimes so Teutonic." She freed her hand and reached under his sweater, trying not to see the black alabaster arm, resting on a block of carved glass, its fingers trailing the air as hers trailed along Albert's spine, one of the fingers wearing a blue diamond ring cut in an oval with a hundred facets.

"I have to know that you accept what I say…" he said, squeezing her hand against his back so it could not move.

Maybe forty karats.

"Fine, fine, I'll never come in here again, I promise."

Albert finally smiled and put her hand back inside his trousers. He pulled her onto a large old red leather sofa, which she had not noticed. He asked Maxine to undress slowly, but to leave her hat on. He liked the wide brim and the floppy flowers.

Maxine took him into her mouth and then into her body, riding him on the leather sofa, twisting her torso so that her breasts in their black lace bra gently slapped his face. Facing her, just beyond the arm of the sofa, was a ceramic Hindu goddess, with grinding hips, and jade earrings, and rose quartz nipples. While Albert was catching his breath, she took a moment to look closely at the extremely large turquoise pendant which hung down into the cleavage of the goddess, suspended there by a platinum chain. Albert rested in her arms. She felt better now. Back in control.

"There is one thing here that I would like to have, Albert," she said. "One thing I'd like us to live with and enjoy every day. And that is the Calder. Please. It's a sin to leave something so unique and beautiful closed up in a vault, when it should be whirling around free in the open air."

He frowned, surprised. It was a look he often gave to Americans. "Well, it makes me very happy to know that you choose this particular thing above all the others," he said. "I don't quite understand why this is what you want, but taste is generally a matter of personal history, and I know so little of yours. Sadly, however, I cannot accommodate your wishes. The Calder cannot be displayed just yet. It needs to be forgotten for some years." And he went to sleep.

This was the first time Maxine had any inkling that Albert possessed things that might not actually belong to him.

Albert slept for 20 minutes, then woke and grinned and kissed

Maxine tenderly. She felt cold and wanted to dress. He had other plans. He covered her shoulders with his sweater. He moved one of the bowls (pink crystal, undoubtedly Venetian) and seated her on one of the little elephants. Her long legs dangled on each side. He took the turquoise pendant necklace off the Hindu goddess and hung it around Maxine's neck. She thought it might be a reward for services rendered, but she underestimated Albert.

The necklace weighed her down. She could barely lift her head. Her hat fell off. Seeing how uncomfortable she was, Albert laughed and rearranged the great chain around her waist. The turquoise pendant rested on her left thigh. He clipped the ruby and diamond earrings to her earlobes, then piled on the gold bangles, then one by one, draped her with the successive strands of pearls. He slipped the huge blue diamond on her finger. Maxine was now very heavy, chained by the jewels like a letter in Erté's alphabet. Albert held her by the shoulder so she wouldn't fall and tilted her backwards and began to rub the turquoise pendant against her sex, looking into her face, smiling a little, his eyes shining with pleasure, not letting her escape, rubbing, rubbing, and she had no choice but to climax in front of him.

You could not win when you played with Albert Vandeblinken.

He only let you hold an advantage as long as it pleased him. Then he took over and had his way.

In that moment of defeat, Maxine decided that it was probably better for her to know nothing more about the objects in Albert's vault, and she averted her mind from them, grateful that he had forbidden her to go back inside because that enabled her to disengage from his other life, his business life, to never think of it. Never.

FIVE.

Advice for a Reluctant Performer

MAXINE HAD ONCE STUDIED WITH an acting teacher, an Englishman, sad from his long American exile. His words came back to her while she was packing for her honeymoon.

"Think of the feeling that you desire to portray," he had instructed. "Then think back and further back until you remember having that feeling and you can recall it with all your mind and body. Then recall the circumstances that surrounded the feeling and summon them, the place, the time, the other people, pull them back with your memory's eyes and ears, and with practice and more practice, you will be able to call up the feeling at will and reproduce it in a different context on stage."

She had never once succeeded in doing what the teacher suggested. Every mood she had played in every medium, from television to romance, was simply a pretense. Pretend misery, pretend happiness, pretend passion. For many years, she had tried, for example, to reproduce the feeling she had experienced when her Uncle Harry in Brooklyn told her that her mama and daddy had been killed by a drunk driver and would never return. Had she reacted with hysterics? Disbelief? Had she felt abandoned? She could not remember.

"You are lying," her teacher said. "You could remember but you refuse to. As a result, I think, you will probably make a good living but you will never be truly respected as a performer."

"I'll take that deal in a minute," she said.

"But you have talent!" he protested. "A real talent particularly for comedy, which often calls on the deepest feelings. Why do you have so little commitment to your talent? You are selfish and shallow not by nature, but *by choice*." He sighed and added philosophically. "An amazing choice. Very American really."

Condescending shit, she thought. Well, fine, fine, so be it. And she remained for the most part a model rather than an actress. She did ads and bit parts in TV comedies and industrials and more ads and expressed the range of her emotions on the stage of acquisition. Getting and spending, shopping and buying, wanting, attaining, amassing, this was the play she had played in her whole life and she loved it, never tired of it, found everything in it from truth to beauty. She still kept the first $100 bill she had ever possessed. It had been given to her for two weeks of modeling swimsuits in a showroom in the dead of winter. It was not salary but bonus, a gift from the management, for her beauty had sold more swimsuits than anyone could have imagined. Maxine put the hundred between her breasts inside her bra, and it rode there, covered with her sweat, as few human lovers would ever be.

"Perhaps someday you will find a state of mind you cannot summon out of your need for security and wealth," the teacher had said. "Some fantastic emotion…so valuable…so precious that it cannot be bought…" He caressed her shining hair. "Will you sleep with me, Maxine, even though I have nothing to give you but advice?"

"Are you kidding? Please…" she answered with a scathing mixture of good humor and contempt.

SIX.

Dinners

ALBERT TOOK MAXINE TO HIS BEACH house immediately after their wedding. On the deck, facing the stars, he embraced her and whispered: "It makes me very happy that you are my wife, Maxine. I wanted you from the moment I saw you." She sighed, contented, for this was what she loved to hear. "Now you must understand one thing, my darling," he continued. "You will have to stop smoking. I have found all your cartons of Marlboros and I have had them destroyed, and the package you set down on the table in the foyer, (he said *fwah-yay*; she loved that too) has been destroyed, and the one in your purse as well. This has been done not for myself but for you, for your health. But incidentally, it is also because the taste of tobacco on your otherwise delicious lips is abhorrent to me."

She laughed and tickled his palm. "Gee Albert, I didn't know anything I did was abhorrent to you."

"Don't try to seduce me, Maxine. You have already done that quite successfully."

He pushed her gently to her knees.

When he was sleeping, she looked and looked for a cigarette. Finally she dressed and drove to town and bought a pack from an all-night drug store and smoked several. On a bridge between two long strands of beach, she got out of her car, tossed the pack into the ocean, then washed out her mouth with antiseptics, mouthful after mouthful, spitting the minty stuff over the bridge railing into the water.

A police car pulled up. "Are you all right, Mrs. Vandeblinken?" the officer asked.

"Yes, of course."

"Your husband asked us to look for you."

"That was unnecessary. I'm fine. I just went for a drive." She smiled. "Thank you for your concern."

"Are you going home now?"

"Of course."

She got back into her car and drove back to the beach house, the cop shadowing her all the way.

Albert naturally knew exactly what she had done and, laughing, hugged her as though she were a little girl. She twisted away from him.

"The thing is, Albert, I really don't want to give up smoking. I enjoy smoking. And even if I give it up, I certainly can't do it" she snapped her fingers "like that."

"Of course, you can," he said. He summoned Greta, the house-keeper he had brought from Zurich. "We'd like some dinner on the terrace." And he specified the wine.

By the whispering ocean, under the starry sky, eating steadily but never speaking while there was food in his mouth, Albert told Maxine about his plan to have a small dinner party three or four times in the season, no more than ten people at each dinner, the guest list to be provided by him alone. In this way, Albert felt he could efficiently offer the hospitality of his new house with its beautiful new wife to everyone he needed to know, now that he was becoming established in America.

"Under no circumstances will you ever tell anyone about these dinners, am I clear? You will never discuss who attends or what was said."

"But this is crazy. The guests will tell."

"No, they will not."

"But I tell everything to Ceecee. And she tells everyone else."

"Not anymore."

"Come on, Albert..."

"I must have your word on this, Maxine." He kissed her ear. "My guests must be able to feel that they can speak openly in my house without fear of being quoted by some journalist."

"Fine, fine, okay, okay, I won't go to the press with transcripts of our dinner table conversation. But please, Albert, be sensible. You've got waiters and waitresses..."

"Greta knows a few who can be trusted as well as a good man to park the cars."

In Maxine's experience, there were no waiters and waitresses in New York (and certainly no parking attendants) who could be trusted, but what the hell, if her husband wanted to cling to a harmless fantasy, let him go ahead and cling.

"So do I ever get to invite *my* friends to our house?" she asked coquettishly.

"Of course, my darling. You may entertain anyone you like — just not at my dinner parties, which are strictly business. Make sure to let me know when you want your friends to come, and I will find an appropriate time in the schedule."

They flew to Italy for their honeymoon. Maxine was frantic. Her hands shook. She snapped at everyone. She became panic stricken because she found herself eating two desserts in one week. She stole smokes in alleys in Bellagio, in the shadowed, swirling stairwells of office buildings in Milan, in the back seats of Roman taxis. But Albert always knew. And he was always angry. The miserable, tortured quality of his anger frightened her. He did not roar and bluster. Smelling the mouthwash, he would simply remove his glasses, sink his face into his hands, rub his eyes wearily, and with a final glance of disappointment in her direction, leave the room.

The last time she smoked a cigarette, Albert confiscated her pocketbook containing her wallet with all her money and credit cards, eliminated the secret caches of cash in her lingerie drawer and her cosmetic kit, and left her alone in their hotel for two days, with orders to the hotel staff not to let her go anywhere, to deliver nothing but the meals he had preordered, and to prevent her from making any phone calls or receiving any from persons other than himself.

To get a taxi to the airport so she could leave him, she had to give her earrings to the maid who sneaked her out of the hotel. She had to give her watch to the cab driver. The police stopped her in the terminal just as she was about to call Ceecee, and they took her to a room where Albert was waiting and, to Maxine's astonishment, weeping real tears.

"Do you want to smoke more than you want me?" he wept. "Is that it? Do you love your cigarettes more than you love me?"

She could have answered him in kind: *If you had any regard for me at all, would you steal my money and monitor my phone calls and imprison me for days?!* However, she sensed correctly that he was weeping to release the emotions that might otherwise lead him (or one of these hired thugs in uniform) to slug her and mess up her face as so many other men had done, and she was past that illness, valued her health now, wanted to live to enjoy her bastard husband's money. She resolved that whatever it took, no matter how much dissembling, no matter how much withholding the truth from her dearest friend, she would live with him in harmony. So she stopped smoking and took up the chewing of ice and the sucking of lemons. And back in Schraalenberg, his business dinners became her life's work, supplanting her career.

MAXINE CONSIDERED HERSELF AN EXPERT HOSTESS. She had given lots of parties for the men and the charities in her life. Her events often made the columns. She had hired and fired dozens of wait staff and cooks, musicians and barmen. However, Albert did not even trust her to order the right flowers. He never allowed her to decide on the menu. Before each gathering, he insisted that the help assemble in the dining room so he could review their uniforms and their grooming. He walked around the table slowly, inspecting each dish and spoon and ringing crystal goblet in the same baronial way he had circled the plane in the hangar, except that what had seemed attractive in the hangar looked ridiculous at home.

Finally, so revolted that she no longer *cared* if he hit her, Maxine said: "You really should stop showing off your catering skills, Albert. All it does is prove to everyone that you used to be a waiter."

Albert did not weep this time. He grabbed her by the throat, making the staff cry out... and then in a flash, he realized that she was absolutely right.

"You are absolutely right, my darling," he said. He kissed her hand. The staff exhaled with relief. A Scottish waitress named Muir slipped a carving knife back into its place.

Thereafter, Albert left the entertaining entirely to her. She fired Greta and replaced her with Muir, who had her own pet waiters and waitresses and one of her own brothers to park the cars.

When Maxine had a party for her show business friends, Albert always prejudged her guest list, vetoing some people who, he felt, tended to receive too much publicity and might talk about the interior of the house – its ebony bookcases, its Rookwood vases on the mantel, its priceless antique hand made Baluchistan carpets – causing thieves to visit.

Maxine saw the wisdom of this approach and went along with it. But once she had a vetted group, she pulled out all the stops. Hot new chefs. Magician waiters. Exotic musicians. Her dinner parties filled Fifteen Willow Cascade with fun and laughter – but not, for Albert, less tension. He just could not feel easy with Americans, much as he wanted to. Their social style alarmed him, made him sly and suspicious. "Too much loud laughter," he complained. "Too much casual touching, too many direct questions."

The business dinners took a different shape. They started at six, ended by nine. Although Albert never told her who was coming and rigorously kept her on a first-name-only basis with his guests, Maxine always remembered what had been served and what she had worn at previous business dinners, so that any repeat customers (there were a few) should be treated to fresh delights.

At a moment of Albert's choosing, Maxine would receive a signal from his eyebrows and, with gracious smiles, claiming fatigue, would say goodnight and go upstairs to bed. Some of the guests would leave soon after. Then Albert would take his remaining company to the back of the house, to what Maxine called The Deal Room, where they would talk and drink and play pool and, Maxine presumed, deal.

She did not ask who had stayed for these meetings in The Deal Room. If she had any inkling of what was being discussed there, she zapped the inkling and never tried to corroborate her hunches. In her pink marble bathroom, undoing her hair, she combed out all memory of the dinner guests, their clothes, the languages they resorted to when English wouldn't say it for them, and drowned out the murmur of voices from below with the rush of her bath water and the gurgle of its soothing jets. She settled back in the scented warmth. Cars pulled out of the driveway. Maxine, who really loved fine cars, stopped herself from playing the beguiling game of identifying them by the sound of their engines and then matching up the cars with the people. Catching a glimpse from her bathroom window, she made a mental note not to notice the make, the model, the plates. By the time Albert came upstairs, the evening was as over and done with as the remnants of food Muir was scraping into the garbage, and Maxine was reading a diverting mystery or sleeping soundly.

In the second year of their marriage, after their eighth business dinner, when the last car had pulled away and Albert was turning off The Deal Room lights and closing its door, Maxine came back downstairs in her rose peignoir to pour herself a snifter of Slivovitz and sit for a few moments on the living room sofa before the fire.

Albert settled next to her, rubbing his eyes. She leaned against him. He put his arm around her.

"Well, that was terrific," she said, "if I do say so myself." He said nothing. She turned to look at him. "You think not?"

"I am tired," he said. "These events are vital but enervating. So much to watch out for. Such an intensity of human interactions. This fellow Bruce, for example, where is his ambition, what does he want? And Richard's wife, was she really flirting with Louis because she liked him? Is it possible for any woman to like Louis?"

"She only flirted with him because her husband needs him for some business advantage," Maxine offered.

Albert chuckled and rubbed her shoulder. "You are absolutely right, my darling. Good that you are here to watch with your American eyes. I do not understand you people, even after all these years. You fool me with your veneer of innocence."

"Maybe some of us are really innocent."

"That is impossible, Maxie."

"But maybe…"

"Have you ever met an innocent person?"

"My Aunt Gladdy…"

"Ah yes, the gentle old socialist who advocated violent revolution. Please." Albert rolled his head back on the upper edge of the sofa cushion. "Some of my new customers are potentially violent," he murmured. "My boy Marcus is afraid of them. He's not very tough. Bit of a playboy, I fear. Shall I fire him?"

"Is that a real question? Do you want an answer?"

"No. I'm sorry I mentioned it. I don't want you to have anything to do with my work."

"Seems to me you might be wise to extend the same courtesy to Marcus," she said.

Albert did not hear her. He was sleeping. His mouth had fallen open. A milky droplet of saliva coursed down among his trim white whiskers.

It occurred to Maxine that Albert might at some point get sick from the tensions of his mysterious business and then die, and the minute she thought that, she realized how much she desired it, and she put the thought from her mind forcefully, the way you close a cupboard when you don't want to eat its cookies, with a resolute slam.

SEVEN.

The Moon Garden

ALBERT'S DEAL ROOM WAS ALWAYS dark. Forest green suede on the walls. Walnut cabinets. A short, massive bar with a mottled brown stone counter faced shelves mounted on a mirrored wall, where heavy carved crystal glasses and square decanters stood in lines. The single bay window facing the back yard was blacked out by thick tweed draperies.

Pictures of dogs brought some relief to the walls. Painted portraits of greyhounds Albert had owned in Switzerland, pedigreed investments that had paid off handsomely. Black and white photographs of New York dogs, captured in mid-frolic by Maxine's first husband, Frank Dash. Albert's dogs stood alone, in Alpine landscapes, their elegant faces haughty. Frank's happy mutts had kids cuddling them and racing with them over the muddy turf.

There was also a montage of photos, assembled by Maxine herself, showing Albert's affectionate life with their dog Hannibal, whom Albert had come to love. They jogged on the driveway together, they lolled on the beach at the Hamptons and posed with Maxine on the windswept deck of a Caribbean boat, the dog copper, the woman bronze, Albert relaxed and laughing, with his hair messy.

During the summer, when Albert was traveling on business, Maxine went into The Deal Room to replace a chipped glass, and she chanced to open the drapes and look out the window. A slice of moon hung low in the sky. The vast lawn stretched all the way back to a grove of silver maples in the far distance, and the moonlight struck it harshly, like an ungelled spotlight on an empty stage. The barrenness of this vista shocked Maxine and left her feeling exposed and endangered.

She stayed up late, devising a plan, making sketches. When Albert called from someplace in Greece, she said: "I've decided to build a garden behind the house. Would that be okay?"

"If a garden will make you happy, my darling, go right ahead."

They had now been married for almost three years, and he had taken to calling her every day while traveling because he found that he missed her wit and her beauty and yes, her occasional wisdoms, as well as the comforts of the home she had created for them. He loved the way Maxine made rabbit stew with thyme and cheese, actually much better than his mother ever had. He loved the way she always had just the beer he wanted on hand, and the way important men in mighty corporations respected him because she was his wife, and the way she placed her cheek at the nexus of his chest and his shoulder and slept, her breath at his throat, her cascading hair on his face, her legs braided with his. Most of all, he loved that she had stopped trying to triumph over him.

Yes, she was a lovely woman, lovely and smart and completely trust-worthy, a real treasure, a prize.

"Bring me a pagoda," she said. "Or a bench. Or a bird bath."

MAXINE ORDERED THE GARDENERS to cut a room in the lawn two hundred feet deep and eighty feet wide. Pathways of white marble chips subdivided the expanse into islands. In some, the crew planted white azaleas; in others, stands of white-flowering dogwoods. She used mock orange as a back wall with a graceful archway in it that led to the silver maples. Wrought iron arches supported cascading white roses and ice blue clematis that overhung beds of white lilies and daisies, lambs' ears and hostas of palest green. On the sunny lawn between the mock orange and the silver maples, there were raised beds for vegetables, the timbers masked by pale stones. And all around, there were daffodils that would naturalize and grow more profuse every spring in great swaths of gold and snowy white.

Of course, all this took a while to settle in and mature. For several seasons, Maxine's moon garden seemed just a perpetual mess in the back yard that Albert never looked at. Then one night, the garden called to him.

One of his business dinners had just ended. He had shown his last guest out the front door and made his last phone call to Marcus in Zurich and had walked back into The Deal Room to turn out the last light before going upstairs. He was having his best year yet. His business was booming. He was farming money now, harvesting money. But he found himself more and more stressed from traveling and buying and selling and suspecting his trading partners, so many of whom were less than honorable people.

Stirred by a kind of ringing in his inner ear, he suddenly pulled the drapes and looked out the big window to the back yard. It was a June night. A full moon. The pale flora that Maxine had planted there shimmered at him like a stage full of ballerinas from a Degas painting.

Albert drifted through the kitchen door and out onto the glowing pebble paths. The moonlight seemed to have entered every flower and every leaf in the garden. He settled himself on a teak bench which he had once sent from Tuscany. The moon shone on the water in the birdbath he had sent from Portugal. He took off his shoes and wiggled his toes among the pebbles. He took off his clothes and stretched out in his silk underwear. The fragrance of the mock orange drugged him. His last thought before being gifted with a refreshing and dreamless sleep was that he loved Maxine more than he could ever have imagined loving any woman, and that he would buy her a wonderful gift very soon, perhaps that silver fox cape she had always wanted, and that it was time to stop having these business dinners, time for an easier, more open life, a life with Marcus and his wife Lin and the children and Maxine's friend Ceecee and her family.

Yes, he thought. Family. That would be good.

part

3

EIGHT.

Advice for A Fatherless Kid

SAM'S MOTHER, ELEANOR EUPHEMIA, made him a big thick hero, wrapped in tin foil, bursting with sausage and peppers and lettuce, every school day before heading out to her job at the diner. If the weather was good, Sam ate his lunch in the sunny spot on the steps of the high school ball field, near the infield scoreboard where he chained his bike. When he was finished, he put the tin foil, with its little bit of leftover sausage crumbs, into the bike basket. His mother, thriftiest of widows, would reuse the foil until it disintegrated.

One day after lunch, Sam realized he had left his locker key in the bike basket and went back to retrieve it. A dog was there, a gray dog with a lot of small round scars on his flanks. He had pulled the tin foil out of the bike basket and was lapping up the residue of Sam's lunch. When he saw Sam, he ran away.

The next day, Sam helped himself to a couple of hot dogs from the cafeteria. He also took a plastic soup bowl but no soup. He chopped up the hot dogs, dumped them in a napkin and ambled outside, trying not to call any attention to himself.

The bike was chained in its usual place. The dog was nowhere in sight. Sam filled the soup bowl with water from a drinking fountain and left it near the front wheel along with the hot dog filled napkin. Then he went off to a sunny spot and ate his own lunch and waited, but the gray dog didn't show.

When the bell rang, Sam had to go inside and upstairs to History. On his way, he glanced out the second floor hall windows toward his bike. The gray dog was eating the hot dogs and lapping the water.

"Look up," Sam whispered. "See me."

The dog looked up. His front legs and his ears straightened. Sam waved.

Every day for a week, Sam left food for the gray dog, who always waited until the kids had reentered the school after their lunch hour before coming to eat his own. On Saturday, Sam rode down to the school and left some real dog food in the same spot. On Monday, when he tied up his bike at the infield scoreboard, the gray dog was waiting. He had two other dogs with him: an untrimmed snow white poodle with only three paws and a large, brown pregnant bitch who was mixed like a salad. They made friends with Sam. They let him pat them. They let him hug them.

To feed this gang on a regular basis, Sam enlisted the help of his best buddy, Charlie Fleeger. Charlie told The Girls, to impress them with how kind and sensitive he was. Soon the whole school knew about the dogs.

"Feral animals!" the principal shouted. "Vermin carriers! How dumb can you be?!"

The boys spent several days in detention. The dogs were never seen again.

Sam's Spanish teacher, Mrs. Artoonian, comforted him on the loss of his dog friends. She was a dumpy woman with a sagging bosom, frizzy red hair and intricate earrings. Her glasses rested midway down her large nose, and the way she looked at you over their top edge made you think she could see right through all your bullshit.

Sam was her best student.

"How did the dogs get here, Mrs. Artoonian?" he asked. "That poodle looked like some rich guy's poodle...that pregnant girl dog had a collar, with her name on it, her name was Pinky. They were like from homes with people. So where did they come from?"

"Look on the highway sometime," his teacher answered. "Watch the cars, and you'll see the people throw the dogs out of the windows."

"That's impossible! Nobody would do that!"

"Didn't you ever see the dead dogs curled up on the side of the road and wonder how they got there? That's how. Murder."

"But why do they do it?! Why?!"

"Dollars and cents, Sam. Think about it. The poodle is pure bred and very expensive and somehow gets into an accident and loses a paw so he is useless for show now and worth nothing. Maybe his owners have insurance on his life but not on his foot so they throw him out of the car to collect the insurance. Maybe the bitch was thrown on the highway because she got pregnant and her owner didn't want a litter of mongrels. The gray dog had been burned with cigars or cigarettes, right? You saw the scars. Well, maybe he jumped out of the car window to escape his cruel owners and because of a break in the traffic or some careful driver stopping short, he made it across the highway and met up with the other dogs and formed a family. So in the end they escaped the fate that had been planned for them."

Sam imagined punishing the evil fuckers who had cast out the innocent dogs and destroyed their happy lives. "They oughta be hung, those bastards," he murmured.

His Spanish teacher peered over her glasses, but not toward Sam, toward something of her own. "Yes," she said. "One could do worse things in life than pursue such fiends to the ends of the earth."

NINE.
The Hunter

SAM HAD HIRED ON as a BIXvan driver after serving five years as a transport specialist in the Army, partly in New Mexico, mostly in Germany. Then he took a course for certification in export management that moved him off the road and into the BIX station at Kennedy Airport in New York. His boss there tended to be cautious, even timid.

On a quiet afternoon, a woman came by who was taller than Sam. She was pregnant. Her name was Shasta Nakamura. A former fashion model, she had quit to marry and raise a family and had recently started a small courier company called Glam Express, which specialized in international small package shipments for the fashion industry. Her company delivered door-to-door in less than 72 hours, guaranteed, to Paris, Milan and London and very often to Tokyo as well, using Air France mostly, sometimes KLM, and cadres of chic on board couriers, actors and models. These people received free tickets from Shasta Nakamura in order to be able to declare the cargo as their personal baggage, with the result that it was off-loaded first before the regular cargo, an invaluable advantage to Glam Express.

Sam's boss didn't like Shasta.

She was too big for him. He couldn't quite tell what race she was. Glittery black hair, short, spiky, maybe electric. Goldish skin, big smile, very white teeth, maybe sharp. She wore exotic Third World jewelry.

She moved gracefully, head held high, as though something precious were balancing up there. The metallic song of her ankle bangles told you she was on her way. As soon as he heard the jangle, Sam's boss said "You take care of her. I've got something else to do," and ducked into the back room.

Sam spit on his fingers and smoothed his moustache.

Shasta said that she had a customer, an assistant buyer at a big sweater company, who regularly shipped with Glam to Paris. But today the French police had asked Shasta to ship the young woman's package with BIX. Apparently, they suspected that this assistant buyer was sending something in addition to sweaters, and they wanted a big company with high tech equipment like BIX to handle her business.

Sam ran it by his boss. The boss said no; these sting operations often worked out badly; someone in the BIX office at De Gaulle might get hurt. No.

Disappointed, Shasta Nakamura turned very slowly, as she might have done in fashion shows past, her long amber earrings gliding past her long neck, and departed.

As soon as his boss went on break, Sam called her and said "No worries. I'll take care of it. I'll swing by your office early AM and pick up your delivery. I'll mark it the way the French cops want it marked and send it in a BIX pouch."

This happened on no less than 11 occasions, giving the French authorities time to learn who was receiving the drugs which the assistant buyer was sending and to track the subsequent street sales. Then they busted the whole ring, including the assistant buyer, who was having a wonderful time at a party in Cannes at the time of her arrest.

"They wreck the lives of people, these pushers," Shasta said. "They should all be armed and sent to an island and left there alone to murder each other."

The French thanked her for her cooperation. They also thanked Jim Brights, who was astonished to discover that BIX had been involved. Who the hell was this nervy bastard in New York making company policy, disobeying a clear directive from his superior, exposing the Paris station to all kinds of dangerous blowback?! Jim flew into Kennedy in a storm.

Sam had just been fired. He was walking out of the BIX office with two weeks' severance in his pocket, thinking about DHL, when Brights leaned out of the window of his chauffeur-driven Chevy and told him to get in.

"I'm listening," he said.

"I couldn't resist her," Sam explained. "It wasn't just that she was hot. It was that she was right. The whole deal was right. And she reminded me of my Spanish teacher."

Jim tore up the severance check. Sam went out to the head office in California. His old boss, humiliated and furious, bad-mouthed him over the years, calling him an underhanded sneak and a ruthless opportunist. That made people fear Sam, always an advantage in any business. He also now had friends in the French police, Interpol and the FBI, and the respect of Shasta Nakamura, whose good opinion he valued.

SAM'S JOB WAS TO TRAVEL from place to place for BIX, to acquire small courier companies with a unique specialty or market zone. Sometimes they fought him, but never did they win. It was the Amman Interavia seizure that caused Jim Brights to make him Director of Strategic Operations for the Western Hemisphere.

Amman Interavia, Ltd. had been established by two former fighter pilots, disciplined veterans loyal to the King. Their company possessed a sprawling network of couriers, many of them relatives, who could handily deliver a package to the most remote localities. Their bankers, also relatives, often forgave a late payment out of simple familial good will.

Generally, BIX used the Jordanians as subcontractors for local deliveries. But then, suddenly, their business got very good. A customer in Mobile had begun sending weekly shipments of videotapes through Amman Interavia to a TV station in Lebanon. The tapes – of American Monday night football games – came replete with nearly-naked cheerleaders cavorting at halftime. In place of the regular commercials, however, there were messages of Christian love. Maybe some other messages also came in the package with the tapes and the love, but

Amman Interavia did not investigate. They delivered by Thursday morning, so that on Thursday evening, few birthday parties were scheduled and even the wars tended to pause, allowing the Middle East to sit down, relax, and watch the Packers and the Giants and the girls.

The Jordanians, sensing a bonanza, raised their rates. The customer in Mobile paid without a murmur. Amman Interavia purchased shiny new vehicles.

Sam flew to Amman. He made the Jordanians an offer for their company. They invited him to lunch and politely refused his offer, expecting that a better one would follow. However, the big American would not play the indigenous business game of meals and drinks and walkouts and comebacks. He had wanted an answer. The answer was no. So he just went home and disappeared for a year.

If his behavior caused discomfort, it was soon forgotten in the ensuing upsurge of profits for Amman Interavia. Kids began to go abroad to study. Wives began to glitter with new jewels.

Sam flew to Paris. He opened a big account for BIX at a French bank, which was the main shareholder in the Amman bank that was backing the Jordanians.

He flew to Tel Aviv and set up a route with a small Israeli courier company, which had vans driven by burly men wearing side arms, in addition to a cluster of Druze bike messengers who could literally hand off a delivery to their cousins on the Lebanese side.

Sam flew to Mobile. He offered the Monday night football customer the same service for one half of the price he was currently paying to the Jordanians. The Alabama customer, sensing a bonanza, demanded even lower rates. Sam agreed. BIX got the account and switched the deliveries to the Israeli route.

The Jordanians, faced with the sudden loss of their biggest account, asked for leniency from their bank. It was no longer forthcoming. Over-extended and burdened with debt, they went broke within the year and sold their company to BIX for a much lower price than Sam had originally offered.

BIX opened a station at the airport in Amman and gave the former fighter pilots baby blue jackets to wear and assigned them to once again deliver American football. The Israelis, faced with the sudden loss of their biggest account, fell to arguing about which of them was to blame for this catastrophe. They finally sold out to BIX for next to nothing just to be rid of each other.

BIX began raising the rates to the man from Mobile. Soon he was paying three times as much as he had ever paid to Amman Interavia.

Deals like these, compounding around the globe, made Sam Euphemia one of the most respected men in the small package delivery business before he was 40. He lived at large, unanchored. Women but no wife, friends but no confidants. He made his home in the belt-like spaces that had lately redivided the world; the acres of containers on railroad car beds that lay inland from the great ports, the cargo-courier cities that skirted every major airport, the phantom corridors of communication that twangled and chattered in the blue air, uniting in a federation of telephones and televisions and computers and satellites that would soon become one galactic machine constituting one gigantic extra-territorial un-country.

While his mother was marrying for the third time back in his home town of Pettyboro, New Jersey, in the VFW hall nestled right under the looming shadow of Garbage Mountain, Sam Euphemia was devouring a good little company in Singapore.

TEN.

Two Deaths

LIKE MANY PEOPLE IN HIS industry, Sam felt greatly concerned about the high rate of accidents among cargo planes. At an air safety conference on the Costa del Sol, he pissed off a multinational gang of officials by publicly condemning the laxity of local security arrangements, particularly for the small carriers.

That night, surrounded by new-made enemies, he decided he'd better not dine at his hotel and took a walk out to the docks to find a cafe. The cerulean sky was just fading into stars. The Spaniards were out drinking. Sam wanted to hear what they were saying. The plastic chairs scraped and tipped on the white tile floor. The gin went down with a pleasant burn. It wasn't too long before he was invited to join a table of Riviera pilots, freelancers who shuffled tourists along the coast in small private planes. They had noticed him at the conference, a powerful American executive and potential ally in their demands for reform of the dilapidated state of nearby runways, the sloppy weather reporting and all too casual inspections. They bought him a drink. They spoke to him in Spanish. They had stories to tell. Sam bought the next round.

One of the stories was about an old friend of theirs, named Hamid. *Hamid flies a regular run in his own air taxi from Tunis to Tarifa. Very windy place. Many windmills for generating power up on the hills. And always big waves on the ocean. So on a day when his own plane is being serviced, Hamid rents a replacement, to fly some young kid surfers to the beach where they will find what will be for them the perfect wave. They are up in clear, blowing weather. And then the landing gear falls off. The plane goes into the water and everybody gets out. The young people who are very great swimmers are racing away from the crash. Our friend Hamid is not so young and not such a great swimmer. They strap him to a board and carry him up and down over the big high waves onto the beach. He dies anyway. He has a heart attack and dies.*

Another foreigner, an Italian who had been hanging at the bar and listening intently to the story of Hamid, asked in a refined voice if there had been an investigation, perhaps a report.

The Riviera pilots laughed in their bitter smoke. Sure, there was an investigation, and a report too, but what could it say? The plane is busted to pieces by the waves, and only a few little bits are found. Simultaneously, each in his own language, Sam and the Italian asked: *What do you think? You the guys who do the flying, why do you guys think the landing gear detached?*

They thought maybe the struts or the bolts and brackets weren't as new as they were supposed to be. But nobody could really tell, because all the papers were in order and the plane had looked just fine. One of the pilots, a grizzled veteran, remarked: "Here on the coast, we call these aircraft 'Sofias' because they look so good, you cannot tell how old they are."

Sad thing, Sam thought, hearing this comment, for a beautiful, innocent woman to have her name made synonymous with a despicable crime.

The Italian bought a final round. He was tall, thin and hollow-cheeked, with a carefully oiled combover. He wore a single gold earring in the shape of a tiny dangling cross. His glasses, dark tinted, gold-framed, gleamed. So did his black, shiny suit. Despite the balmy night, he sported a white silk scarf, imprinted with roses, that hung open with a Hollywood panache. His hands, pale and hairless, had polished nails.

The only less-than-stylish thing about the Italian was on his feet. He wore large black blobby shoes that looked to Sam like they had been prescribed by a physician.

He handed out his card to everyone. Inspector Vito Branca. From Verona.

Sam hissed from behind his teeth, shook his head and smiled self-deprecatingly. He had not spotted the Italian for a cop.

Inspector Branca was interested in the crash of Hamid's plane because it reminded him of other mysterious crashes he had been looking into. In fact, he had come to the air safety conference in search of just such a story. For his part Sam wanted to know about those other mysterious crashes. They left the cafe together and found an empty place where no one would overhear and talked, in Italian, over a dinner that lasted until dawn.

In the months that followed, Sam Euphemia and Vito Branca became close colleagues. They stayed in touch regularly through channels that often included the French police, Interpol and the FBI. They shared crash files, investigative reports, interviews with survivors and witnesses on the ground.

The precise and determined Branca came closer than anyone to verifying Brights' Lunacy. He tracked down the Frenchman who had rented the plane to Hamid. The Frenchman said that he bought it at auction in Algeria. The Algerian auctioneer checked his records and found that the seller was another Frenchman, who had offered small planes for sale before. This second Frenchman, corpulent, talkative, said he had bought the plane in Italy more than ten years earlier, from a broker representing a Swiss company which, this broker had claimed, had connections to lots of reconditioned aircraft.

Branca immediately set out to interview Marcus Vandeblinken in Zurich. But before he could get there, Marcus was shot dead on his own doorstep by a drive-by assassin. When the Swiss authorities finally allowed Branca access to Marcus' papers, he could find no record of the sale of any plane resembling the one that had caused the death of Hamid.

part

4

ELEVEN.

Sweet Pea

THOSE BRIGHTS INTERNATIONAL employees who were responsible for compiling information about Maxine paid scant attention to her relationship with the bootmaker, Ceecee Blochner. They found Maxine's ex-lovers much more compelling. The judge. The producer. The drug company president. Thus, they wasted a lot of time and energy snooping in empty corners.

Maxine Klein met Celestita Rodriguez when they were both eight years old in the desert town of Sweet Pea, Arizona. It was 1939. The Depression had begun to ease but still burned in everybody's memory.

Maxine's Aunt Gladys taught at the Indian School on the reservation. She had a barter arrangement with Celestita's older sister, Rosita. Gladys would teach Rosita how to read and write English and Spanish, and Rosita would do the laundry and clean the house and make sure that, when Maxine and Celestita came home from school, they drank a glass of cold lemonade with one or two of the cookies which Gladys often baked and which Rosita called "roogaloo."

The neighborhood ladies did not initially like Gladys. She had come from New York on a Wednesday. She attended labor union meetings and was suspected of being a communist. Some folks wanted her fired from the Indian School where she was rumored to be teaching the kids to be dangerous revolutionaries.

Then Maxine arrived, along with the story that she had lost her folks suddenly in an accident. Her mother's brother, Uncle Harry in New York, had two boys of his own to care for in these hard times, so that left Gladys, her dad's sister, to raise Maxine.

No one in Sweet Pea believed this story.

No one believed that Rosita Rodriguez was Celestita's big sister either, but no one cared. As far as the neighborhood ladies were concerned, she was just another wetback girl who had come north alone with a kid in tow. Somebody had told her that if she admitted how she had really gotten the kid, the baby might be taken away and given up for adoption, whereas if they were sisters, they might be adopted together or better yet, left alone.

Luckily that was what happened. They were left alone. Rosita cleaned and mended for all the neighborhood ladies. She had a boyfriend on the reservation.

Every morning, Celestita would leave the room in Horny Toad Alley where she and Rosita lived and pick up Maxine at Gladys' house, and they would walk together to school, laughing and singing and dancing like Ginger Rogers and Fred Astaire in the dusty road.

A short, strong girl with rounded arms and a wide smile, Celestita moved fast, her thick, black, chunky braids bouncing against her shoulder blades like soft brushes.

Maxine too had black braids in those days. Hers were long and silky, like ropes, and her gait was slow and dignified. Her braids didn't bounce. Rather they gently swayed.

She had once lived in an apartment with a radio and a piano so she knew lots of songs: romantic ones *("Blue heaven and you and I...")* and tough ones *("We are the peat bog soldiers...")* and zany ones *("Sons of pork and gravy, Join the Yiddish navy ...")* She could imitate John Wayne, Marlene Dietrich and each of the seven dwarfs.

Celestita possessed more practical gifts. She ironed well, never a wrinkle remaining. She set the table with the forks and knives exactly straight and equidistant from the table edge. When Rosita got sick, and Gladys made her some chicken soup, Celestita served it on a tray with cactus flowers in a vase fashioned from a bleached bone she had found in the desert and a cloth napkin sewed from the remnant of a torn shirt and folded to look like a bird.

Maxine often dreamed to Celestita about the wonderful life she would have when she went home to New York. She would have a big apartment overlooking Central Park where she would live with her wealthy husband. She would have lots of cute little children. Every night, she would tuck them up all snuggly in their beds with comforters and fluffy pillows and bring them hot chocolate and read them stories, just the way her Mama had done with her when she was little.

"Tell me about the hot chocolate," Celestita said. "Tell me about the comforters and the pillows."

Maxine would describe the tawny sweetness with marshmallows foaming like white caps on the surface, the brocades and velvets, the shams and their fringes and little feathers flying free.

Celestita never talked about her old home in Chihuahua except to say that she and Rosita would not go back. Their mom was dead. They had never met their father. Rosita had worked in the fields for a man she had come to hate and had run away with Celestita in the dead of night.

"I was just a baby then, so I do not remember this running," Celestita said, "but I know for sure we are finished with there."

Soon the neighborhood ladies smiled and waved as the two girls passed, their black braids bouncing and swaying. Soon they began to believe that Maxine really was Gladys' niece, that the awful story of her orphaning – her mama and daddy laughing at breakfast, gone forever by lunch – was actually true. Soon everybody in Sweet Pea was calling Celestita "Ceecee", as Maxine did.

In the evening, when the stars were hidden by clouds and the desert was so black it seemed like an ocean, the girls would sit with Gladys and Rosita on Gladys' front porch, the women sipping beers, the dinner stew softening in the pot, and they would sing *La Paloma* and *Streets of Laredo* and *Hard times, oooh hard times, come again no more…*

A stray mutt came out of nowhere to enjoy the music and lay panting at their feet. They fed him and petted him and named him

Nowhere. When a tarantula visited, he chased it away with wolf-like ferocity. He killed snakes and scared off unwelcome gentlemen callers. "Ah darling Nowhere, how lucky we are that you stand guard for us," Gladys said. "You are our Lion of Judah." She scratched his ears. He lay his head in her lap.

Gladys always told Ceecee that she was beautiful. "You are our Aztec queen," she would say. "Look at what perfect brows you have, like the wings of the hawk soaring."

She didn't have to tell Maxine. By the time she was 12 years old, Maxine knew. Everybody knew. Everybody could see how beautiful the lanky kid from Manhattan was becoming, how enticingly her heart-shaped behind trembled inside her dungarees.

Gladys felt uneasy at the way people looked at her niece. There were so many lonely men in town, brought to Sweet Pea by the Federal flood control project. It was a great relief to her that Officer Nacky kept coming around on his big horse, Chico, "to check up," he said with a polite smile, "just to check up on all these pretty women with no one to protect them but some stray dog." Grateful for Nacky's concern, Gladys made him welcome in her home and served him the eastern delicacies that she baked in the cool of the night.

Nacky was a small man, wrinkled and rutted by the sun and the wind, and his brilliant blue eyes had narrowed to slits from squinting. He wore a deputy's badge and a khaki uniform. Daily he rode down the main street of Sweet Pea, patrolling the dusty storefronts, and then out to the reservation, which went silent at his approach.

ONE WEEKEND IN THE LATE WINTER, when there was some rain to be had in the desert, Gladys decided to build a training farm in her yard, to teach the children the skills she felt they would need to participate in the new world order that was sure to come once fascism had been defeated for all time.

She tied up her hair in a bandana and put an old straw hat over it. She showed Maxine how to measure out the beds with little stakes and lengths of red string, assigning each variety of vegetable and flower its special homeland. Then, with some of the Apache kids to help, she demonstrated how to pulverize and turn over the dry earth, and she unloaded barrows full of sheep shit among the clods. Maxine raked and raked the grassy turds, to spread them evenly among the plant nations. Soon she had blisters on her palms and a nut-brown complexion.

Every day after school, the many children of Gladys Klein worked on the training farm. They crept on their hands and knees along the red tie lines, digging irrigation troughs among the rows, all the troughs interconnected in a maze. No sooner had they finished than a passing shower sent thin rivulets of water racing among the beds, and the kids cheered.

Rosita did not allow Ceecee to join in this work. When the workers were thirsty, the sisters brought water; when they were hungry, they served sandwiches; but they did not go out to plant.

"Rosita says it is bad work for a woman to be in the fields with the tall corn all around," Ceecee quoted. "So we do not work in the fields."

"To work in the fields is how you become a free person," argued Maxine. "Aunt Gladdy says that's how we've got to learn to live now, in farming clans like our ancestors did. Everybody will work in the fields and each of us will give in what we can and take what we need and there will be no envy and no greed and no crime."

"Sounds like a lot of hooey to me," said Ceecee.

As the vegetables and the flowers grew on the training farm, people in Sweet Pea felt a little more lighthearted. Sometimes some citizen would just wander alone into the garden and pull some weeds and crouch by the sprouting lettuce in a reverie. A Navaho girl on a painted pony stopped to pick a bouquet for her mother. A young woman with not enough supper at home to feed her many kids took some tomatoes, and an old drunk took a couple of peppers. Rosita wanted to ask Officer Nacky to run off these poachers, but Gladys said to let them be, the earth and its fruits belonged to all the people.

Officer Nacky often rode by on Chico and joined the neighborhood ladies as they watched the progress of the work on the training farm. He observed Maxine bending over in the budding beds of lettuce and eggplant and peppers. He observed Ceecee with her water jug and her basket of sandwiches, as she passed among the rows of workers, then sitting on a boulder and making sketches of them on her big pad with her soft charcoal. Good girls. Hard-working, helpful girls.

Nacky's own son could help with nothing. He had returned crippled from the war with Japan, and the girl he had planned to marry had dumped him, and now he was living home with Nacky and the Missus, dependent on them and those they could hire, angry and distant.

"Isn't it always like this?" Gladys commiserated, shaking her head as she poured coffee for Nacky in her kitchen. "The robber barons use the wars for their own profit and the courageous sons of the working people pay the price."

As soon as there was a crop to harvest, Gladys organized a celebration. She called it "First Fruits." Everybody was invited: the small farmers who had bought the old spreads for cheap from the bank and were now bringing them back to life; the kids from the reservation and their mothers, even some of their fathers; the bow-shaped cowboys; the migrant vegetable pickers and their families; the young girls who had found work in the re-opened cannery and wore new dresses made by Rosita, who now had a sewing machine of her own. Some of the men from the Federal flood control project arrived, and so did the neighborhood ladies who had once felt so suspicious and kept themselves so remote. A Mexican band showed up and just played.

Ceecee and Maxine did their own special rendition of *Let's Face the Music and Dance,* which they had seen at the movies. The graceful, languid Maxine was Ginger; the shorter, more sure-footed Ceecee was Fred.

When was the last time any of the folks in impoverished Sweet Pea had seen anything as beautiful as Ceecee and Maxine dancing?

On a Sunday after returning from church, Officer Nacky asked Gladys if he could take Ceecee and Maxine for a ride on Chico, just a slow ride down the main street of Sweet Pea, he said, just for fun, for a special treat since they were such hard-working, helpful girls. The girls were delighted at the idea and wanted to go. Gladys couldn't resist their pleading and said sure, that would be fine.

Off they went, Nacky walking in front, leading his horse by the bridle, Maxine riding frontways on the saddle, Ceecee sitting behind her, their backs pressed against each other. It was a Friday afternoon and the laborers from the construction projects and the boys from the traveling rodeo were all in town for a decent meal and some female company. Chico walked slowly past them, swatting flies with his tail, taking care not to stumble because he was carrying innocent kids who didn't know much about riding horses.

Soon Nacky had handsome offers for each of the girls.

Rosita learned this from one of the neighborhood ladies.

Gladys refused to believe it. Nacky was her friend! Their protector! How could such a betrayal be possible?! She burst into tears. Rosita told Gladys to stop crying for Chrissakes and get real for once and figure out how the hell they were going to escape.

Nacky summoned the Immigration police. They inquired at the school, looking for Ceecee Rodriguez. Her teachers said she had not been around for some time, but the Mexican kids were like that, coming and going as the seasons changed.

When the officers showed up at the homes where Rosita had been accustomed to work and displayed their deportation order and demanded that Rosita and her little sister be sent out so they could be loaded into the truck full of illegals bound for south of Nogales where they belonged, the neighborhood ladies smiled and said that Rosita had not worked there for some time, not since her boyfriend had returned from France, and they had heard that she married him and they took her sister and went west to the coast to work in the shipyards, or maybe a restaurant, and the officers should look for her in San Diego or Seattle.

Nacky called the FBI and led them to Gladys' house. She wasn't home. They easily opened her door and confiscated cartons of incendiary propaganda about Native American national pride, the Mexican cultural heritage, the rising of the masses, the rights of the workers, more than enough to get Gladys fired from her job, maybe even detained for a few days in jail. Nacky had figured that a few days was all he needed to deliver the goods and collect the fee.

However, Gladys and her beautiful niece could not be found. The neighborhood ladies variously offered that they had gone to Phoenix to work for a dry cleaner, or was it Portland? Out at the reservation, the people murmured that Gladys had probably returned to her old home back east and Maxine with her.

Nacky sat himself down in Gladys Klein's abandoned house, deeply disappointed that his promising plan had come to nothing. In the back yard, the training farm was bursting with its first fruits. Many citizens harvested there, although they were careful to leave plenty for the poor folks, who were embarrassed to need so much and would not harvest in daytime in front of their neighbors but would surely come later to glean in the moonlight.

The old policeman sighed. Sometimes you just couldn't catch a break. He poured himself a glass of nice cold lemonade from Gladys' refrigerator and ate the last of her indescribably delicious rugalach.

TWELVE.

The Journey to the East

GLADYS HIRED SOME WRANGLERS WHO owned a horse transport to spirit the girls out of Sweet Pea. These were men whose families had enjoyed Gladys' hospitality. She taught some of their children. They were her friends. They promised to deliver Maxine and Ceecee to the station in Tucson and put them on the train to New York, where Maxine's uncle would take care of them.

The girls rode with the horses, hidden by their big bodies, feeding them the apples and carrots Rosita had packed for them.

On a deserted side road, the wranglers pulled over, "for a drink and a stretch." The girls sat with them. They felt safe and comfortable with these fathers of kids they knew. But soon there were attempted caresses, and the girls became frightened and pulled away, twisting and kicking. The men laughed and grabbed at them with powerful hands. Maxine pushed Ceecee behind her and magically produced a knife and threatened to hurt them if they didn't back off.

The friends of Gladys Klein, ready for fun but not for trouble, threw the girls' little suitcase out of the van and just drove away.

So there Maxine and Ceecee stood, on a road in the desert. Nothing to do but walk back to the highway and hitch the rest of the way to Tucson.

"Where'd you get the knife?" Ceecee asked as they trudged through the dust.

"Rosita gave it to me as a goodbye present. I've also got matches and mercurochrome and band aids."

"Why didn't Rosita give *me* a knife? I'm her sister for Chrissakes!"

"She said you were too nice, that I'm meaner and tougher. You got the wallet as a goodbye present from Aunt Gladys, because she thought you were better with money."

She was referring to the wallet that Ceecee wore on a rawhide thong around her neck. It contained all their funds for the trip as well as their train tickets.

"What are we going to do now?"

Maxine responded firmly. "We are going to look for water and a town where we can buy food, and we are only going to accept rides from ladies."

It took a full day of walking before they found a lift with a ranch woman driving a pick-up, and by then, they were very hungry. She gave them water and chattered about how hard it was for a woman to keep things going until her husband could finally muster out and come home from Okinawa. She dropped them at a gas station. It had nothing to eat. The girls were now dizzy from hunger, a feeling they would never forget.

A woman and her mother pulled into the station. They took ten cents from Ceecee for the leftover half of a peanut butter sandwich. The woman would have given the girls a lift, but the old lady said no Mexicans. No.

The girls split the half-a-sandwich and walked on. Sometimes they couldn't find an acceptable ride for a long time, and they had to walk for miles. Night came.

They built a fire, as much to alert passing cars who might rescue them as to keep away the creatures. Maxine slept with the knife rolled up in her coat, which she used for a pillow. Ceecee slept on her belly, with the wallet flat against her naval and her head against their little suitcase. In the morning, they washed up in a crystal river.

They were famished.

A Mexican family took them to a tiny little store at the corner of two roads. The clerk, Miss Lila, had skin as polished as a river stone. She wore the most beautiful earrings Maxine and Ceecee had ever seen – silver, set with turquoise and cat's eye. Lila took them off, so the girls could see them up close. She said they were a gift from her father-in-law, Mr. John Silver Smith, whose other works – bracelets and lockets and silver-studded leathers – were displayed for sale in the little store. Lila was 16 and pregnant. She let them feel the baby move inside her.

The girls bought some food and cokes from her and then for a while, they all sat on the porch outside the little store, eating and chatting and waiting for a passing car to give them a lift. The traumas of the previous day seemed so remote in this peaceful place that Maxine packed her knife away in the suitcase. Lila gave them each an extra coke, no charge.

Soon, two ladies in a nice car stopped by the store. One lady had curled golden hair and spectacles. The other lady sat in the back seat with a bag of groceries.

"Can we be of any help to you, girls?"

"Oh yes, ma'am," Maxine said. "We just need a lift to the train station in Tucson."

"Well, that's exactly where we're going. How fortunate! Get in."

Overjoyed, Maxine climbed into the back seat; Ceecee, clutching the suitcase, into the front. They all waved goodbye to Lila Silver Smith.

The blonde lady drove straight down the highway toward the city for a while, then suddenly veered off into a network of dirt roads, through a mesquite thicket, past a broken gate where an old frying pan still hung, past a tall cactus with its arms broken off, onto a little bridge that crossed a moist riverbed and into a wasteland.

Maxine leaned forward. "Where are we going?" she asked. "Is this a short cut?"

The blonde lady laughed, reached over and opened the passenger door, shoved Ceecee out of the car into the dirt and speeded away. Ceecee scrambled to her feet and raced after the car, screaming for Maxine who was screaming for her and struggling in the grip of the woman in the back seat. The car disappeared.

BLOOD FROM A CUT ON CEECEE'S HEAD ran into her eyes. She stood in the desert, howling for help. Then she collapsed in tears. Then she dried her eyes. She tried to be like Rosita and get real and think

She did not know where she was. Maxine was stolen. In a few hours, it would be dark. But still Ceecee had the wallet hanging around her neck concealed inside her shirt. And she still had the suitcase. Broken by its fall from the car, contents sprawling, but still...

Ceecee gathered up their stuff, rammed it all into the suitcase whose halves she tied together with a belt. She put the knife in the waistband of her dungarees. That was a comfort and steadied her mind. Praying for the right direction, she began to retrace the route of the car, looking for the bridge across the river bed, the amputated cactus, the frying pan at the gate, the mesquite shade. It took her an hour to get back to the highway. And just as the day turned pink and aqua with one of Arizona's glorious picture postcard sunsets, Lila came by, riding next to her husband, who had picked her up at the end of the work day in his wagon. She told him to stop, because that filthy, bleeding, exhausted girl in the road was an acquaintance of hers.

Lila remembered the two ladies and their car. As it would turn out, her husband knew exactly who they were and where they lived and the man they worked for. He would not call the police. He said the police were likely friends of that gang and would not turn over a white girl to the care of John Silver Smith's family.

Lila's husband drove his wagon to a pretty cottage, with a white fence and horses in the yard and lace curtains. When Lila knocked on her door, the golden-haired lady opened it eagerly. Clearly, she had been expecting somebody else.

"That is her," Ceecee said. "She is the one."

The woman turned and ran. Lila caught her and held a hatchet to her throat

Begging for her life, the blond led them into the basement. Maxine was sitting on a bed, hugging her knees to her chest, her face hidden and her hair streaming down all around.

They had put her into a yellow dress and tied yellow ribbons in her hair. Her feet were bare. The grocery lady was guarding her and knitting.

Ceecee began to cry. Maxine did not cry. She was finished with crying.

Lila wrapped her in a blanket and helped her walk upstairs. Lila's husband told the whores to stay in the room. He closed the door and pulled a heavy table in front of it, so they couldn't get out. But anyway they wouldn't have tried to get out because they were so afraid of Lila and her hatchet.

The girls stayed almost two weeks with the Silver Smith family. Lila's husband got in touch with Rosita and Gladys, who were hiding out at a commune in Oregon where Gladys had friends. Gladys called Maxine's Uncle Harry in New York.

Lila's father-in-law showed Ceecee his workshop and all his tools. Lila's mother-in-law burned the yellow dress. Maxine listened to the radio. Nobody, not Lila or her husband or his parents, not the whores or their pimp or the doctor who saw Maxine, ever called the police.

THE WALLET THAT GLADYS HAD GIVEN to Ceecee was beautiful, entirely embossed with a design of flowers and leaves, the outline of each petal tapped into the leather with a tiny chisel and a delicate hammer, then filled in with intricate filigrees and curlicues. Ceecee took care not to let anyone but Maxine see the wallet. However, when they had finally seated themselves on the train to New York, she let down her guard for a moment. Maxine was staring out at the tumble weed as it raced by the train, her eyes almost all black, her mouth calm and dry. Ceecee wondered: would Maxie ever laugh and sing again? Would the bruises on her arms and legs ever go away?

On her sketch pad, Ceecee began to make a picture of her friend. When the conductor called "Tih-ketts!", she was so engrossed in her work that she retrieved the tickets from the beautiful wallet without trying to hide her treasure. The money, 11 single dollars, peeked out.

Eleven dollars. Not nothing in 1946.

"Nice picture," the conductor commented.

"Thank you."

"You girls traveling all the way to New York?"

"Yessir," Ceecee answered.

"You sisters?"

"Yes, we are."

"One Mex, one Merican," he laughed. "You sure got a mixed-up family."

Maxine turned from the window. "Our family is none of your business," she snapped.

"Hey, no problemo, just being friendly." The man tipped his official conductor hat and moved on through the sparsely settled car.

The girls had been given some food by Lila and her mother-in-law, and it was just about gone. They expected to be able to get off the train the next morning when a long stop was scheduled and buy milk and bread and cheese; maybe a melon, some apples, even a fruit pie. So they carefully divided their last piece of bread, their last tomato, the last of their milk, sure they would be able to fill up at breakfast, and fell asleep leaning on each other.

When they woke, the wallet was gone.

They searched all over for it, inside and under the seat, on the floor. Some other passengers helped them with the search until their own stop came, and they had to get off. By noon, they had looked everywhere. No wallet. Two days to go. No money. And once again, they were starving. Ceecee began to cry.

"I want to go home to Sweet Pea!"

"We can't," Maxine answered. "It's too dangerous there."

"It is dangerous everywhere! These people, they are like mountain lions! They just jump on you and boom! They eat you!"

The remnant of the rawhide thong on which the precious wallet had hung slipped out from under the collar of Ceecee's shirt. It fell from her neck like a little dead snake, the ends neatly cut.

"It must have been the conductor," Maxine said. "He was the only one who saw it."

She had a look on her face that Ceecee would see again many times in her life. Deadly determination. Frozen heart.

"Are you going to stab him with your knife?"

"I don't know yet."

Maxine washed up and combed her hair and went to find the conductor. She walked and walked through the cars, aware that many men looked up from their lunch sandwiches and beers to admire her. At each coupling of the cars, the train track flashed up with a terrifying glint, but she did not coddle her fear, she pressed on, looking for the conductor, describing him to anyone who would listen.

"That would be Burt," said a porter pulling suitcases down from the rack.

"He stole our money while we were sleeping."

"Well, even if that is true, young lady, and I'm not saying I disbelieve you, you are out of luck because Burt got off this train four stops ago."

Maxine walked slowly back toward Ceecee. A soldier met her in the aisle and, laughing, played a little game of not knowing which way to pass. Although she was seething with anger and desperate for something to eat, Maxine made herself smile shyly at him. "Wow, what a looker!" she heard him comment to his friends as she walked on.

She found Ceecee washed up and neat, hard at work on the charcoal portrait of Maxine that she had begun the day before.

"I need the dress." Maxine said.

Ceecee opened the dusty little suitcase and pulled out their one dress. It was a shiny purple frock with a full skirt and short sleeves and a scene of Hawaii – palm trees, hula girl, island moon – painted on the bodice. A neighborhood lady had given it to Rosita at Christmas, and she had outgrown it. So in fact had Maxine. When she emerged from the bathroom, wearing the dress, Ceecee shook her head and said: "It is no good. You are pushing out too far in front. The dress is going to tear."

"Do I smell okay?"

"Yeah."

"How's my hair?"

"Okay."

"I'm going to go and get some money. So we can eat. Don't be scared if I'm not back for a while."

"What are you going to do?"

"Just stay here. Don't go off any place."

"Maxie…"

"It'll be fine."

When she returned an hour later, Ceecee was not in their seat. Maxine became terrified for the first time during the long hungry day. Something white and thick seemed to fill her chest. She could not breathe. Her eyes closed. She felt that she might not be able to open them again. *Where is my friend, my defender who saved me from the terrible basement?! Where is she?!*

Then Ceecee came scampering down the train aisle with her sketch pad, wearing a big grin.

"I went into the next car and I showed the people my picture of you that I made. And they thought it was pretty good. So they asked me to make a picture of their little boy. And they liked it pretty good, so they gave me 25 cents for it! And then some other people who saw the boy's picture wanted me to make a picture of their grandma. So I did. And people kept on asking and I kept on doing pictures and now we got two dollars!"

"Four," Maxine said, holding out two crumpled singles. Ceecee's eyes welled with tears. "Now don't start crying again. It wasn't like that. I met this soldier and we were talking and okay, yes, I offered him me for a couple of bucks. He said okay and we went in the bathroom. I took off the dress."

"I do not want to hear!"

"Okay," said Maxine.

She sat down. Ceecee couldn't stand that.

"What happened?!"

Maxine smiled. "He undid his pants and then my stomach made this loud sound. Like this. *Urrrr…nhhhhhnhhhh…Grrrr Grrr…..uh-h-uh-uh-uh mmmmmmm uh-uh….*"

"Maxie!"

"So he did up his pants and gave me two dollars, because he said he had met too many starving kids in Italy who were ready to fuck him for lunch, and he was finished with starving kids."

Ceecee glared at her. "Is this a lot of hooey? You just telling me this so I will not feel bad about you becoming a who-err?"

"C'mon, let's move into a really crowded car."

After that, Maxine and Ceecee kept their money in their underwear. Occasionally somebody would come by looking for the little Mexican artist girl, and Ceecee would do a portrait. She was proud of herself. She really was. But she never forgot the beautiful wallet that Gladys had given her. The slashing pain of having it stolen – a matchless object, made by hand, *by hand!* – oh, the loss of it stayed in her bones. Harsh reminder. Mountain lion.

To Maxine, the theft of the wallet and the sad comedies that followed on the train from Tucson proved only that Ceecee was the one with the talent, and that she had nothing to sell but herself.

THIRTEEN.
Husbands

CEECEE TOO FELT THAT SHE and Maxine had been programmed by the farewell gifts they had received as kids in Arizona for the roles they would play in later life, that she had been chosen by her wallet to be the businesswoman, keeper of the estate, the creative, clever one, but personally defenseless. When she felt threatened by anything at all – a dissatisfied customer yelling, a storm with lightening, a daughter not returned home on time – she experienced a sharp pain at the front of her head, as though she were being tossed onto the dirt road again and her head was smashing against a rock and there was blood in her eyes.

What if Maxie had not threatened the horse wranglers with her knife? What if Lila had not held her hatchet to the whore's throat? Ceecee could not endure these "what if?" thoughts. She had to have her own weapons. She gravitated toward big, physically powerful men, carpenters from the theatres, grips and gaffers whom she met on movie sets where she worked as a seamstress and costumer when she was young, men with instantaneous access to dangerous tools.

She believed in the right to bear arms. Her company often gave money to gun lobby candidates, and Ceecee herself had a permit to carry. She sent her two daughters to karate classes. Gladdy became a black belt.

Ceecee refused to live in a house, recalling the pretty cottage where

Maxine had been imprisoned. That house, so innocent behind its neat fence and lace curtains, with the good hearted horses grazing nearby, that house was Ceecee's nightmare. "No houses," she instructed her husbands. "No houses ever. I want to live in a building, on a middle floor, with neighbors all around and above and below. And I have to have a fierce dog who will stand guard like our dog Nowhere who watched over us in Sweet Pea and who will suspect all strangers and attack anyone who means to harm me or mine."

CEECEE'S SHARPEI, PUPU, WRINKLED as a lava bed, folds upon folds of tan flesh rippling on forehead and jowls, had been picked up from a litter, advertised on a bulletin board in a union hall, by Ceecee's first husband, Waldo, a scenic designer. When Waldo left her for someone he thought he loved more, PuPu stayed with Ceecee. He guarded his mistress and her black haired girls with jealous ferocity, growling and snarling like a killer at any stranger who was not personally introduced and vouched for. He returned lost toys to their cupboards. He brought Ceecee her *Wall Street Journal* and her *Women's Wear Daily* and her slippers and sometimes her lost reading glasses too.

"You are the best doggie-woggie in New York," she said, hugging him, and he basked in her love, broad smiles hidden by the folds upon folds. He adored her. He adored the Latin flair that made her eyes sparkle and her shawls spangle. Every morning he lapped up a cup of black coffee to please her (she said it would jump start his day). He grew to relish a splash of salsa verde on his kibbles and bits

As Ceecee's leather goods business grew, she rose in New York's culture crowd. Friends of one of the smaller opera companies invited her to attend a benefit. She looked great that night. She wore white boots decorated by appliqués of beaded red flowers and a long black lace skirt and an embroidered blouse cut to reveal her plump shoulders and the northern slope of her large breasts.

At this benefit, services and luxuries were donated by generous supporters, then auctioned off to the well-heeled crowd. You could bid for such things as tickets to *Carmen* plus dinner for two, or a car for the weekend in Santa Fe during the opera season. Ceecee bid on and actually won a motorcycle tour of The Five Towns on Long Island. The tour was offered by a beefy merchant named Herman Blochner, owner of a landmark hardware and lumber outfit that served the theatres in the west 40s.

Like Ceecee, Herman worked personally in his business, right on the floor with the customers. On sunny weekends, he liked to put on his old leather jacket and his helmet and ride his roaring motorcycle around the community where he had lived unhappily with his first wife. He did this to annoy his old neighbors. *(Crap! Here comes Blochner again on that goddamned Harley!)* If he could also have a pretty woman behind him, clutching his belly as he thundered by, all the better.

The day that she was supposed to ride the Harley, Ceecee changed her clothes four times. She did her hair up, she did it back, she did it down. She was clearly nervous. That made PuPu nervous. When the buzzer sounded, Ceecee ran to open the door. She found Herman Blochner nervously spritzing breath spray.

She drew him into the living room, talking softly, her eyes gleaming behind their shiny lashes, and she did not even introduce him to PuPu. No best doggie-woggie. Not a word or a glance.

PuPu felt very hurt. It was late summer; the girls were away at camp, which meant he had no one to cuddle him and make him feel better. Hoping to create a criminal record that would force Ceecee to pay close attention to him when she came home, he left his toys all over underfoot, barked viciously at the evening dog walker whom he knew and liked and usually licked, and finally peed on the carpet. But Ceecee didn't come home until very late, and by then PuPu was cuddled up asleep in his soft bed.

Later on, he awakened, shook out his folds and padded silently into the living room. He saw Ceecee on the sofa, and Herman's ecstatic face, and that was the way it was forever more.

PuPu witnessed first nine-year-old Gladdy, then 11-year-old Rosie transfer their thwarted Daddy-love to Herman. Toward the end of his days, when PuPu could not even muster the strength to make the once easy leap into the Volvo, Herman picked him up and carried him, saying "Don't feel bad, old fella. We all deserve a little TLC for our long years of service. You especially, you who took care of my Ceecee when she was all alone, you especially…"

Thus, even jealous, possessive PuPu came to adore the great love of Ceecee's life, Herman Blochner.

HERMAN DID NOT LIKE Albert Vandeblinken.

Ceecee pointed to Albert's poise and good taste, emphasizing that his appearance on the crowded stage of Maxine's love life had ended the horrible abuser phase. But Herman didn't like him. Although Maxine did not report a similar aversion on Albert's part – he hardly noticed Herman and really didn't care one way or another – the two couples rarely socialized.

However, when Ceecee and Herman had been married for 14 years, Maxine and Albert for six, and it looked like both marriages would last, Ceecee decided to push for a joint holiday. It was just too freezing in New York, she said. She and Maxine had a hankering for the Caribbean. Accepting a clear inevitability – how could he deny her something she wanted so badly? – Herman agreed to a vacation at a complex of posh villas on the French side of the island of Ste. Maarten in the Virgin Islands

Herman liked to slather himself with lotion and lounge about in the sun while reading political biographies. The big gold *chai* that nestled half-hidden in the curly gray hair of his chest often left a white imprint on his tan. He would flop and splash in the ocean, tossing the whooping Ceecee into the waves. Or he would play sloppy games of volleyball with strangers on the beach, sand and sweat spraying. Then he would shower and sleep and make love and drink banana daiquiris and eat the local fish fry and take his gleaming brown wife in her white lace and silver to the casino to shoot craps.

Albert dressed in gauzy pale clothes. He avoided the sun between ten and three. He rode horses on the beach in the early morning, then swam laps in the private pool at his villa, enjoyed a salad lunch with other businessmen with whom he had become acquainted, and played tennis in the late day.

By contrast to this precisely scheduled set of activities, he and Maxine made love on whims of the moment and thus often at inconvenient times. They might be all dressed for their night out, ready to go, and she would adjust his tie, and he would kiss her shoulder...and that would be it.

Eventually they would catch up with Herman and Ceecee at their rollicking crap table. Maxine would go off to play black jack or roulette. Albert observed the games, but he never gambled.

On one occasion, when the day had come in a bit cloudy and the women had decided to go shopping in Marigot, Albert and Herman found a couple of wicker rockers on a verandah and actually talked for a bit, drinking gin and lime.

"My father was an innkeeper," said Albert. "Mama cleaned. I waited on the table and hauled the garbage. The war brought us German and Italian deserters. They gave Papa beautiful things they had stolen. In return, he would obtain forged papers for them, sometimes sell them a companion for an hour, and then smuggle them into the mountains so they could disappear.

"I remember, one night, Papa laid out all his loot on the dining table. Money, china, silver, bolts of silk, old books and many jewels. Mama couldn't look at it. She wanted to get rid of it right away. He said patience. Wait. Wait for some years. Then we buried it. I did the digging."

Herman whistled. He lit one of his big cigars. Albert did not protest.

"When the war was long over and the value of things had begun to inflate, Papa started cashing in his treasure. He became prosperous. By then I had my license, flying the commercial routes. I had already discovered that the profit in aviation was to be made on the ground. I needed cash to take advantage of a good deal available in Sicily. So I went home and convinced my dear father to give me his money."

Herman asked: "Do you think your dad would have been a smuggler and a pimp and a purveyor of stolen goods if there hadn't been a war?"

Albert looked up from his drink, not at all offended. "What an interesting question," he said. "I honestly do not know the answer."

"Ceecee loves to work," Herman said. "But I swear, she'd spend her last dollar not to have to clean her own house."

"Ah, well, but of course, this is natural," Albert responded. "Since Rosita scrubbed so many toilets."

"What?"

"Did you not know that?"

"I thought they all worked in the leather business. Their father had a tannery. He went bust and sent the girls north."

Albert laughed regretfully.

"Herman. Please. What father?"

"In the 50s," Albert recounted, "when Papa became so wealthy, Mama left. She hired herself to some people in Virginia as a housekeeper. I visited her there. *Mein Gott,* Herman, such bounty. So many peaches and tomatoes and automobiles and fields of green grass just for grazing horses.

"My mother's employer rode out in the morning on his brown mare, and I thought, now this is real wealth. To own creatures who bring you no food and do no work for you, totally unnecessary creatures, just for show and pleasure. A horse from a noble line. A pedigreed dog. A lovely woman who does not dip her little finger into dishwater.

"I wanted very much to take my mother out of service and set her up in comfort in London where I had my office then. However, she would not leave her job, her 'freedom' she said. A job as a servant, and she called it freedom. She loved America."

"Me and my first wife, we really didn't want a divorce," Herman said. "We really wanted to kill each other. But I couldn't take out a contract on her because the only criminals I knew were thieves, not murderers." He waggled his eyebrows and chortled, expecting Albert to laugh too at what was obviously a joke. But Albert only nodded thoughtfully and sipped his gin.

"You have known my Maxie longer than I, Herman. Tell me, will she ever be satisfied that she has amassed enough wealth?"

"Never. Too insecure. Too much happened to her when she was young. I mean, imagine, to lose your folks that way, in a split second. To be snatched off a road and dragged into a brothel and raped…"

"What?!"

Herman winced and said "Oh shit."

MAXINE SETTLED INTO A QUIET GAME of black jack. She looked especially beautiful to Albert that night. She had taken to wearing her hair in a coil at the base of her neck. She wore chunky gold earrings and on her upper arm one of the bangles from his vault. It clasped her like a slender vine, and the swelling flesh around it was soft and tempting. Her concentration on the cards caused her to pass her tongue over her lower lip, causing her lower lip to glisten. It pleased him to watch everyone noticing her when she slipped onto the chair and put her money on the table. They were trying to recall where they had seen her, he knew that. Remembering her name and how beautiful she had been. Noting how beautiful she was still.

Albert passed behind her, resettling her shawl around her shoulders. Without looking, she reached back and touched his hand, and everyone could see that she belonged to him.

A police captain from Michigan, turned to an African darkness by the island sun, sat at the end of the table on the right. He played with cautious pleasure, beating the dealer just enough to stay in the game. Next to him, a lady who was probably much younger than Maxine but who looked many years older owing to her obesity, drank scotch rocks, wore purple lace and displayed over her cards a foot-long cleavage. Next to her, a medical student on his honeymoon, his burned nose shining with emollient, pouted unhappily. He had lost all but his last stack of chips, and the night was young. Next to him, Maxine. And next to her, at the left-most chair, a used car dealer named Buddy.

Buddy was losing hand after hand and drinking steadily.

Maxine was winning. Her pink fingernails clicked against the pink chips, and the ice in her mouth clicked against her white teeth. When the dealer gave her two kings, she split them and doubled her bet, and turned, looking for Albert. "Stay here by me," she said softly.

The police chief was dealt a jack and a seven. Madam Cleavage pulled on 14 and held on 18. The honeymooner bet his second-to-last $50.00 and held at 17. Maxine received a queen to go with one of her kings and a six on the other.

"A small one," she told the dealer.

He dealt her a five.

"Twenty-one for the lady."

The three people to Maxine's right cheered and applauded good naturedly at her excellent luck. Buddy showed a jack, pulled a six and then an eight. The dealer whisked his money away.

"That was my five you took," he griped nastily to Maxine.

"Excuse me?"

"You pulled on 16. Nobody should do that. I would've had a jack and a five and then a six but I didn't because you stole my 21 by pulling on 16, and that meant I had to pull on 16 and I pulled over."

"I never heard anything quite so idiotic in my life," Maxine said.

The dealer was already handing out new cards. The honeymooner had withdrawn, reducing the table to four. The police chief, the purple lace and Maxine were all dealt picture cards. Buddy got a three, then a six, then a four, then a queen.

"Fuck!" he yelled. He slammed the table so forcefully that a green drink with an umbrella splashed all over the purple lace. "You fucking bitch, you stole my luck!"

"Look what you did to my dress!" cried the splattered woman.

"What dress was that, lady? I didn't notice you were wearing one!"

The woman burst into tears.

The police captain, whose gifts included an ability to tell by the least word or posture exactly when a dispute became dangerous, merely smiled and shook his head at this raucous exchange. But when he heard the white-bearded foreigner say quietly to the much younger Buddy *"You had better apologize to the ladies immediately, sir"*, the cop leaped to his feet, stepped between Albert and Buddy and did not relax until the security people had taken the unruly drunk out of the casino.

Ceecee came racing across the floor when she heard the commotion. Maxine assured her that everything was all right. Like the police captain, Herman knew better. He had recognized the malevolent charge in Albert's voice as he demanded an apology and noted his lifeless smile as Maxine tried to placate him: *It's nothing, darling. Please don't upset yourself. Please, Albert.* Herman knew damn well the incident was not over.

So he was not surprised when, about six weeks later, Maxine told Ceecee that suddenly, out of the blue, the idiot from the black jack game in Ste. Maarten had sent her a set of sterling silver candlesticks from Tiffany with a note of apology. A saleswoman she knew there reported that the same gentleman had sent identical gifts to three other parties besides Maxine, including – and this was information the saleswoman certainly should not be quoted as having given – Mrs. Somebody in Terre Haute and Captain Somebody in Detroit and the manager of a casino in Ste. Maarten.

Strangely, Maxine seemed not pleased by the gift but disturbed by it.

"Let me tell you something, sweetheart," Herman said to Ceecee. "When I was serving in Korea, we were attached to this Turkish unit. These guys carried fancy daggers with their regular kits. If you asked one of them to show you his dagger, he would do it. But he'd prick your finger to get some blood on it before he put it back. That's Albert, baby. A fancy dagger. Force him out of his cover and he won't go back unless he spills blood first.

"Think about putting some distance between yourself and Maxine, baby. She's not living with a high type guy."

FOURTEEN.
Marcus

IT AMAZED MAXINE THAT HER marriage to Albert had mutated from a financial deal enlivened by good sex to an actual love affair, replete with devotion and tender concern. No more business dinners. Lots of visits with Marcus and Lin and the kids. Wonderful summer evenings of grand opera at L'Arena in Verona. Being Mrs. Vandeblinken was turning out to be quite a nice ride.

He hung the multicolored pearls with their diamond clasp around her neck. He wrapped her in the fabulous fox cape he had bought for her. He took her to an opening at the Met in New York, and the women in the audience sighed with envy. She loved that. Afterwards they went out to dine with friends. It was nearly two o'clock when the car dropped them at their home. Eight o'clock in the morning in Zurich.

Albert's son, Marcus Vandeblinken, walked out his front door to feel the weather, to ascertain whether his children should wear extra sweaters to school. He loved his children. Loved his chic, smart Chinese wife, his sure-footed polo ponies. He adored his father. He regretted that he would never possess his father's iron-fisted negotiating style and business acumen. But then again, Marcus thought, Albert had grown up in a war zone, a merciless world that required a man to be much more heartless and combative than today, and a car drove past and someone in it shot Marcus in the head and killed him instantly.

Returning to the rotunda of Fifteen Willow Cascade, Maxine

swirled her cape around Albert and pressed herself to him and kissed him, filled with gratitude for the pearls and the fur and the box seats at the Opera and the delicious dinner and her terrific life. Then the phone rang.

LIN VANDEBLINKEN BURIED HER HUSBAND as quickly as possible, gathered up her kids and as much of her money as she could, fled to her father's house in Hong Kong and hid there, leaving everything else she possessed behind for the Swiss police to examine.

They found nothing that would definitively solve the murder. Vandeblinken employees in Zurich and Newark were questioned again and again. The visiting Italian police inspector, Vito Branca, received special permission to scrutinize every piece of company paper. Nothing. Since Marcus was known to be a good customer for certain illegal substances, and one of his suppliers had already been killed, the murder was ultimately laid at the feet of the cartels, and the books were closed.

At Fifteen Willow Cascade, friends descended like a swarm of wasps and nested there, besetting the anguished father with their sympathies. When they left, finally, Albert fell to pieces, howled and smashed the mirrors of the house with his fists, unable to look at himself, making his hands bleed.

Day after day, he closed himself up in The Deal Room, pacing, phoning, pacing. When Maxine knocked on the door, he snapped at her.

"Yes. What is it?"

"Dinner. Food."

"Not now. Go away."

At night, he clung to her.

"Tell me," she whispered.

"No."

"Please."

"Quiet."

He rolled over onto her body, attempting to touch as much of her as he could, wriggling and swimming in her hair. She tried to push him off so she could look into his face and know his thoughts. He would not be moved. He stayed flat upon her, an implacable weight. Maxine wrapped him in her arms. She absorbed his tears into her skin.

She reached out to his first wife, Marcus' mother.

"Thank you for calling," said that poor lady. Her voice from London sounded like a voice from the moon. "But I can be of no help to Albert. He is alone with this."

Maxine began taking Albert to grief counselors and psychiatrists. She took him to churches and synagogues. A young rabbi invited them into his study and spoke about family and history. Albert wandered around the room, antsy, fidgeting. Finally, with an impatient groan, he simply walked out, leaving Maxine to apologize and fluster.

The rabbi gave her a lift home.

"Do you know why Marcus was killed?" he asked.

"No. I assume some drug deal or something."

"Do you think that Albert blames himself?"

"Yes. I suppose he does. He always feared that Marcus was a lightweight, in over his head with people he couldn't handle."

"Do you think that now he is afraid for his own life?"

"I don't know...yes...maybe...I don't know."

The young rabbi pulled up to her gate and waited for Muir to open it from within.

"Listen Maxine," he said. "You want my advice? Stop schlepping Albert to shrinks and spiritual advisors. He's only keeping these appointments for *you*, because he loves you, to make you feel useful in his time of grief. But he will not be comforted."

part

5

FIFTEEN.

The Buried Man

SAM EUPHEMIA FLEW INTO KENNEDY after a long, hard sojourn in Venezuela and Brazil. He had not heard a guileless word in weeks. He felt stuffed with lies, sluggish from the weight of them. Needed a little pick-me-up, some honest laughter and good company that would sympathize with his cynicism. So he headed over to Wally's Old Bar. It was three in the afternoon on a cold day.

A dark, one-story building, outfitted inside with an antique tin ceiling and real wood floors, Wally's stood at the nexus of a dilapidated post-war highway and the sleek marginal cargo road that now encircled the airport. Here the air courier industry met to exchange news of hirings and terminations, buyouts and takeovers, political upheavals and accidents. As one of the very last structures to survive the demolitions that had recently transformed the area, it served as an historic marker for folks who remembered Idlewild, the Lufthansa heist and the Brooklyn Dodgers, who could recall the days when local kids went clamming in the sandy shallows and raced headlong beneath their soaring kites, when the streets were safe and the air as fresh as the morning's catch.

Over the years, the ocean inlets around Wally's Old Bar became dumping grounds and choked on garbage. The shellfish beds lay smothered. An oil company moved in with its storage tanks, crenellating the horizon. The water thickened. The fish disappeared. The airport spread.

Mind numbing noise overhead and chemical stenches, never before smelled in human history, made life intolerable in the little towns. Criminals moved into the now valueless houses, transforming them into stashing and forwarding points for drugs and weapons and kidnapped children. So, in Sam Euphemia's era, when the great cargo and delivery companies took up residence in their spiffy new glass office buildings, they were actually, as Shasta Nakamura had once put it, "lying down in the same stinking landfill with the enemies of humanity."

Sam checked in at the bar; met some colleagues; heard some gossip. The mirrors all around him revealed Shasta in a booth at the back. She was talking to a man who wore a mink hat with earflaps. Clearly a business meeting with one of her eccentric fashion industry clients.

Sam had heard that Glam Express was doing well these days. So well in fact (his assistant, Siloo, had learned this from a model who often traveled as a Glam courier) that Shasta had been emboldened to finally throw out her scurrilous Wall Street husband and file for divorce.

The guy with the mink hat was leaning toward her at their table. Obviously pitching her some idea. She was leaning back, distancing herself from his proposal, her long arm in its gray sweater sleeve draped on the bench top, her nose held high, connoting that she was far from sold. Sam could see her fingers dangling, the fourth finger relieved of its ring. He could hear the occasional chime of her bracelets. It looked to him like an important meeting. He did not interrupt.

But when Shasta turned to speak to a waiter, she noticed Sam at the bar and, with a smile that said he was just the person she wanted to see at that moment, she beckoned to him. Sam spit on his fingers and smoothed his moustache, took his drink to the booth and sat down next to her warm hip.

"This is Mr. Zapata," she said. "He has an interesting idea. He wants me to organize a refrigerated shipment of something called 'The Sugar Maple Orchid' to Tokyo in April."

"Orchids don't grow on maple trees," Sam said.

"That used to be true!" agreed Zapata enthusiastically. "But no longer. These orchids are like a phenomenon of the crazy new weather.

They grow right out of the branches when the spring comes and disappear in the winter."

"Hard to believe."

"Wait until you see. The orchids are extremely delicate; they must ride the whole way in the refrigerator."

"It's already very cold in cargo, Mr. Zapata." Sam said.

"Ms. Nakamura has told me exactly this. But I must insist on extra precautions. We must have the orchids in perfect condition for the big show in Tokyo."

"The flower show?"

"The sportswear show," answered Shasta with a grin.

Zapata suddenly leaped up onto the booth bench, his earflaps flipping with excitement. "You must imagine this, Mr. Euphemia. Roomsized video projections of snowy woods. Mohawk drums dadum dadum dadum. A voiceover speaking Japanese with a thick Maine accent that says 'And now, ladies and gentlemen, here comes Mr. Zapata's fabulous North Coast Collection! Newport regatta whites and storm-proof slickers available AT LONG LAST! in super petite sizes for the modern Japanese woman!' Imagine the astonishment, the thunderous applause as the teeny tiny models sail down the runway in their thigh-high hard black rubber Gloucester fisherman boots and each one carries a perfect purple orchid raised on the bark of the Vermont sugar maple, symbol of the forthcoming millennium when all plants grow in all soils in all countries in all climates and all women get to wear whatever they want, no matter where they are from, or how teeny tiny super petite they are! Oh God oh God! It will be a sensation!"

Shasta laughed. Her earrings jingled. An irresistible music.

Sam arranged for Glam Express to ship the "Sugar Maple Orchids" in the refrigerator on a BIX plane to Tokyo in time for the sportswear show in the spring. They were, as Mr. Zapata had predicted, a sensation. The Bennington nursery which had piggy backed its innovation on Zapata's designs was soon flooded with Japanese orders.

Preparing for this success, Shasta Nakamura had assembled all the authorizations, licenses and clearances necessary for transporting horticultural and agricultural products across state and international boundaries. Back in California, Sam heard that she had opened, with some fanfare, a new office at Newark Airport, from which she not only operated Glam Express but also a spinoff company called Flora Shipments International.

Then some prominent horticulturist told a Tokyo fashion magazine that these orchids were not indigenous to New England at all but a hoax, an ordinary tropical variety raised in a Hawaiian garden, then sent to Vermont and pinned onto the limb of a sugar maple long enough for a photo shoot.

Sadly, Shasta shelved her new agri-licenses. Of course, she should have known better. People in their business had to understood about fraud and misrepresentation. Customers and couriers alike constantly practiced the arts of falsification. Packed prescription drugs in vitamin bottles. Tore the tags off new jeans and called them old. They had all been taken; they had all gotten away with more than they could ever admit.

They spent their days bringing order and direction to the delivery of things, sanctifying schedules, re-verifying weights and measures, calling ahead, calling yet further ahead, and still they knew in their hearts that every safe arrival depended ultimately on luck. Luck that the plane took off; that it landed; that the baggage handlers didn't go on strike; that the consignee didn't go bust before paying; that the check cleared. Good luck that your thigh-high hard black rubber boots went over in Tokyo. Bad luck that an expert on tree-borne orchids from Maui happened to pay special attention to an unusual credit card payment his stylish wife had made to a plant nursery in Vermont.

Sam sent Shasta an email. "It was a good try. Sorry for your loss. I'll be back in New York Thursday evening before another trip to South America. Do you have time for dinner?"

Shasta figured that this invitation presaged the end of her business.

Leaving her regular bling at home and dressing with what she thought would be appropriate conservatism for her dinner with Sam, she told her father, who was babysitting, that BIX was about to make her a next-to-nothing offer for Glam Express and its spin-off, Flora Shipments International, both now in desperate financial straits. Maybe, if she was lucky, Mr. Brooding Man-of-Few-Words Euphemia would also offer her a job.

To her delight, that did not turn out to be what Sam had in mind.

HE LEFT NEW YORK FOR A COUNTRY where BIX was having some troubles. A new strongman had seized control of several major cities and ensconced himself in a palace on the edge of the jungle. The national government appeared to be powerless against him. Having killed so many people, this strongman, a drug lord, proprietor of whore houses, international trader in priceless tropical birds that were supposed to have been safely protected, now feared that everyone was trying to kill him. Therefore, he bugged all the phones. Read all the letters. He wanted to open all the packages too and threatened to arrest any courier who tried to deliver anything in his territory unless it had been searched and approved beforehand by his enforcers.

Sam was tasked with negotiating a deal that would protect BIX staff and customers from the new regime. He had a substantial budget for payoffs.

The local BIX station manager, a watchful, pudgy man, picked him up at the airport. They set out in his van for the strongman's palace. They came to a military roadblock. At gunpoint, Sam was forced out, blindfolded and handcuffed. As he was being shoved into a truck, he could hear the pleas and protests of the station manager, he could hear the thud and groan as the bastards pistol whipped the poor guy and left him bleeding on the hood of the van.

For 62 days and nights, Sam was imprisoned in a cinder block room. The walls wept with liquid heat. Only the slimmest glimmer of light crept in from the single small window. No messages came from his embassy or his company. When rats approached, he beat them to death against the wall and sent their bodies back to his guards on the food tray. Though therapists would ask him repeatedly, he would never be able to fully describe the panic that overwhelmed him in that stinking, airless hole. He felt as though he were being melted. The heat seemed to be burning his skin to tatters, which the jungle damp and his own sweat would then wash away, leaving him flayed, crystalline as an amoeba, all innards showing.

His boyhood stared out.

He could not stop thinking about his father, Angelo Euphemia, dead at 32 in an explosion at the landfill called Garbage Mountain. Sam heard the rumble that Angelo must have heard. Felt the geologic shudder under his feet. Clawed at the air as the earth swallowed him. He recalled a monster in a movie who digests his victims forever. That's how Sam felt in the cinder block room. Endlessly swallowed, suffocated, endlessly fighting for his father's last breath.

He could not stop thinking about his mother, Eleanor, the hero maker, a woman he had erased from his mind for years.

She had started trying to get married again not two years after Angelo's death. One candidate thought her little boy was cute and played with Sam. The rest ignored him.

When Sam was 12, Eleanor succeeded in capturing a surly, hard drinking teamster. It was a big sexy thing, thrashing and moaning right down the hall, and Sam hated to be around it. He escaped as much as possible, slipping from the house in the dead of night and riding his bike out to the Turnpike. There he would walk on the concrete median like a tightrope artist, with the 18-wheelers whirring along on each side of him, and the planes roaring overhead, and the cargo heists of the great port creaking and grinding, until the cops pulled him off and forced him to go home.

Eleanor, sound asleep in her husband's arms, usually never learned about these episodes. But one night, she and her husband were not sleeping. Instead, they were having a fierce argument when the highway patrol dropped off Sam and his bike. Eleanor felt so embarrassed in front of the cops and guilty at not having realized her son had been absent without her knowledge that she flew into a rage and screamed at Sam. He screamed back, calling her terrible names.

His stepfather hit him until his brains rattled.

This kind of beating happened once more. The boy was late coming home from a party. The man was drunk. Eleanor was helpless. The third time, however, Sam, now 15, decked his stepfather and stood on his chest and wouldn't let him get up off the floor. Eleanor roared with laughter. The marriage ended, and the hunt for Number Three began.

At school, Sam daydreamed about Italy. He imagined distant relatives in sun-bleached olive groves, holding out their arms to welcome him. Repeatedly he asked his mother if they could visit someday, and she always said sure, someday, maybe.

He worked summers in a garage. With his money, he bought "Learn Italian!" tapes. He wrote to his grandma in Sicily, imagining her sweet gray bun, her baggy black dress. She never wrote back. But Sam kept on writing, sometimes to the old lady, sometimes to his father's brother, Joseph. Once he tried to reach the family by phone. Joseph Euphemia in Palermo had an answering machine that asked the caller to leave a message and Sam did, but no one called back. He tried calling again and again, with the same result, and never found out if the silence in Palermo was Uncle Joseph.

Eleanor said: "Oh for God's sake, stop this hunt for the stupid Euphemias. They were just jerks. Your father was the only good one. You don't need them. You got your own life."

But Sam felt that he did not have his own life, that the mysterious foreign relatives were hiding it from him.

He took a tramp vacation in Europe with his best friend, Charlie Fleeger, and some other Pettyboro guys. In Rome, he cut away from them and went to Palermo and rang a bell that he was sure would open the door to the Euphemias. The people there remembered Joseph. They said he had moved north years before. But whether to Milan or Norway, they did not know.

He found a Joseph Euphemia in Milan. The man spoke high-toned, university English. "Ah, how I wish I could be your uncle, my dear fellow," he said. "I could pretend, and you might believe me. But something as important as family must not be disguised, don't you agree?"

Upon Sam's return from his Army service, his mother made a big welcome dinner. The third guy, a thoughtful plumber, was there at the table. She served her wonderful osso bucco to him first, before Sam, because she wanted him to marry her. Her hair was orange. She had a black line around her eyes that made her look like a target. And she said right out at the table: "Biggest mistake of my life was using Angelo's settlement money to pay off my mortgage. But I had bad advice from my dad. He was a Depression person. He thought if you own the house free and clear, the bank can't take it back from you in hard times, and you've always got a roof over your head. The Euphemias never forgave me. They thought I should have shared the money with them."

Sam had asked her for years why the Italian family wouldn't talk to them, and she had never before said it was because of some money. *Dollars and cents, Sam. Think about it.*

"Why didn't you tell me that, Ma?"

"Because I didn't want you to think badly of them, just in case they ever showed up. But now they're all of them dead, so who cares?"

"Now they're all dead?! When did they die, goddammit?! How did you know they died?!"

The plumber slipped away into the kitchen, taking his plate, so that mother and son could fight in private. Neither noticed his departure.

"I got a postcard from Joey when the old lady went. He wanted money to bury her. He was always like that. Looking for a handout from his rich American sister-in-law, the widow of the construction worker. Then I got a postcard from one of the cousins when Joey got killed, in some accident I think but I can't remember now, it was a long time ago."

"You got postcards! You knew when they died, you knew there were cousins, and you didn't tell me! Why didn't you tell me?!"

"Because it was ridiculous the way you were hunting for them, calling them and writing them, the way you left your friends, didn't even go to see the Vatican, Charlie Fleeger told me, traipsing off to Sicily looking for those bastards."

"I needed to know them!"

"Well, they didn't want to know you!" she shouted. "They thought

Angelo would get rich here, and when he didn't, they hated America. And that included us. And that's the truth, honey!"

She knows the truth, right? This ignorant woman, didn't finish high school, doesn't read a newspaper, never voted in her life, lives like a slut and prays to Jesus for forgiveness and then lives like a slut some more, she really knows how Angelo's family feels, how Angelo's son should feel!

Sam slammed out of the house on Rumble Street, vowing never to return.

However, his success modified the vow.

He began sending money, larger and larger amounts as the years went by, until finally the plumber wrote and asked him to stop, they were doing okay on their own and if he really wanted to put things right with his mother, Sam should send himself instead of a check.

Over and over in the cinder block room, he heard the explosion at Garbage Mountain. He saw his father plunging into the pit, heard him screaming, and to keep himself from screaming too, he began to sing.

Sam sang every song he could think of, all the lyrics mashed together. *Pajama rolled out welcome to the Hotel move these refrigerators salut demeure chaste et holy night the stars are sock it to me sock it to Georgia! Georrr-jah just for the taste of sea to shining...* When he lost his voice, and could only croak and wheeze, he still sang on. *Only the good die verrrry good year...*

The guards threatened to shoot him if he didn't shut up. Sam knew the threat was empty, because he understood their language and he had heard them discussing the orders they had been given not to harm a hair on his head. So he sang on.

Una furtiva lagrima...ya da da da da da da....

One morning, an American diplomat came, flanked by the dictator's soldiers but not scared of them, reaching for Sam's hand and pursing his mouth in a cautious *Shhh*. Sam would have hugged him and kissed him but restrained himself because he did not want to appear unmanly before his tormentors. However, the blast of sunshine outside the prison knocked him into the dirt.

The diplomat helped him to his feet, whispering "It's okay it's okay, I've got you..."

When he arrived at Kennedy, Sam learned that Jim Brights had personally paid off the strongman to get him out, and that BIX people at all the stations in all the airports had held prayer meetings and sang hymns to convince Heaven to save him, drowning out the prayers of ill will that came from those who felt he had wronged them, the Jordanians and the Israelis and the evangelist from Alabama who worked for British intelligence, and the European air safety bureaucrats whom he had publicly attacked and his old boss, the timid one, who had long since left BIX but would never forget the humiliation he had suffered there.

Sam's mother and her husband were waiting for him at the airport. Jim and Siloo and a lot of the other BIX people he knew were openly weeping. He saw Shasta Nakamura, half hiding herself on the outskirts of the crowd. Her face was haggard with worry, her lip bitten, her eyes blurred by tears of relief to see him whole and home again.

It was the glimpse of Shasta – she cared about him, an accomplished, principled woman, a woman with her own problems, she had really cared whether he ever got out of that hole – which made him soften and accept his mother's embrace and her tear-soaked kisses.

"I thought of you all the time in there, Ma," he said, in a graveled voice almost destroyed by singing.

SAM NEEDED A VERY LONG TIME to recover. That surprised him. He had thought he would bounce back.

He took a vacation on a balmy beach but found no real solace. He detested himself for his nightmares and his need for chemical help to calm down and his inability to conceal his distress.

His reputation for toughness, so laboriously fashioned, began to crumble. His ravaged voice became a growl. His eyes strayed from the subject at hand. He didn't want to sleep, in case he should dream, and staggered bleary eyed to work. Several times, hearing some noise, he stomped on a rat who wasn't there. He was, for the first time in his life, impotent.

Siloo would find him standing perfectly still in his office, transfixed in a flashback, staring at what appeared to her to be nothing. When she spoke to him, he did not hear her, so deep in was he. Knowing how determined Sam had always been to find the corrupted aircraft called Sofias, how fascinated with any material pertinent to the Vandeblinken murders, she brought him a fat dossier about Maxine, which had been prepared by Detective Meeker. It included a large coffee table book of photos entitled "The Art of Frank Dash: Humanizing Nature." Here were the famous photographs, now museum pieces, that Dash had made when Maxine was a girl. Roses on her breast, one thorn pressing but not piercing. A purple iris tilted downward on her hip, its spiky leaves clasping her waist. Limp tulips resting on her thighs. The flowers seemed so comfortable in the vases of Maxine's body that the pictures weren't even sexy.

"Remind me again who she is," Sam said.

Jim Brights anguished over his suffering protégé. Sam's thinness, his trembling hand and distracted eyes tore at the older man's heart.

How could he have sent his most companionable manager, his confidant and clear successor, his best-loved boy into such obvious danger?! How could he make amends for allowing such an outrage to occur on his watch?

Jim could see that being locked up in a rat hole for two months had taken a toll on Sam far beyond remediation by shrinks and vacations. He was too shaky and insecure now to handle his former responsibilities. He needed a different job, more suitable for someone who had been through hell.

"All right now, listen, this is what's going to happen," Jim said. "What's going to happen is that you're going to move out of Acquisitions and hug the ground for a while. I'm making you a vice president of this company. You're going to be our philanthropic arm. We should have had one long ago.

"Go back to New Jersey. Get yourself a house, maybe by the ocean, fresh air, plenty of space. Plant our money where it will do some good and make people love us, and you. Very important change here, Sam. In this job, people are going to love you.

"Make Mrs. Vandeblinken one of your projects. Get to know her. Get to know her friends. Check out the charities she's involved with. See what's buried in her garden."

part

6

SIXTEEN.

Advice for a Businesswoman

SHORTLY AFTER ALBERT'S DEATH, Ceecee had treated her company's courier to a working lunch at a restaurant by the East River.

"What a horrible thing, I read about it in the papers, about your friend Maxine, her husband, murdered, my God...," Shasta Nakamura said, never dreaming that this might be an incendiary remark.

"Screw horrible," Ceecee replied venomously. "Albert was cheating on Maxie with some little who-err and her thug lover blew them away. They got what they deserved."

Shasta was shocked. After all, they were both sophisticated women, admirers of Hillary Clinton. "Come on, Mrs. Blochner," she said humorously. "That's much too harsh. Being an adulterer is not like being a crack pusher. If all the old men who had stepped out on their wives were killed, there wouldn't be any grandpas left."

Ceecee leaned toward her, eyes narrowed, arthritic fingers with scarlet nails drumming the table. "I could take my account to BIX at any minute," she said deliberately. "Right now. Right now. I could make one single phone call and all your hard work, your connections and systems that you have developed just for Rodriguez Fancy would be finished. You would be finished. Why do I not do this, Shasta? Because you have performed well for my company and I feel loyal to you. Loyalty is everything. Without loyalty, there is no safety. We could never take an easy breath. Without loyalty, we would all be road kill."

The frightened courier, one third of whose business depended on the Rodriguez Fancy account, had begun to sweat.

"Now," Ceecee continued. "Let's talk about our shipments to Milan."

SEVENTEEN.
The Widow

Most of the people who were watching Maxine after Albert's death would not have imagined that she grieved for him. But she did. A phrase from an aria could swamp her with memories. She brought the happy Hannibal pictures upstairs to live on her bedside table, then added a more recent one of Marcus and Lin's children playing with their Grandpa and his dog in the beautiful moon garden of their Grandma Maxie.

Daily she received visitations from the police, the FBI, aviation officials and aircraft industry people purporting to have been Albert's close friends. Many of her old show business buddies, whom she had entertained so creatively as Albert's wife, came by to comfort her. She felt somewhat pissed that no one who had stayed late in The Deal Room after one of the business dinners ever showed up. Apparently, silence was a double-edged sword. You didn't speak of them. They didn't know you.

If visitors forced her to discuss Albert, she did not weep – hell, she had not wept since she was 13 years old – but her voice grew softer and softer, so that people had to strain to hear her. Finally she lapsed into total silence and just stared helplessly at them until they gave up and went home.

When at last she was alone and could crawl into bed, she slept in Albert's clothes, in his smell.

The identity of Albert's murderers meant nothing to her. She figured anyone could have killed him. Crooks. Customers. Customers who were crooks. Competitors. An angry husband or lover as Ceecee contended. It was possible that people inside his own company had assassinated him and would soon begin shooting each other. Fine fine, let them go at it. Their bloody work had nothing to do with her. She was out of it, immaterial, unconcerned. All she wanted was to survive this period of forced public mourning, collect her inheritance and enjoy life. Patience, Maxie, she counseled herself. Soon. Soon enough. Patience.

For months she went to the gym, went shopping, lunched with friends, waiting for the estate to settle, the snooping to end. She puttered among her flowers. She started putting hundreds of old pictures into new albums, carefully recording the date and the time and the occasion.

Detective Meeker, forever hitching his belt and jingling, goaded her with questions about that unfortunate woman whose severed hand had been tossed onto Albert's body. *Did you know your husband was cheating on you, Mrs. Vandeblinken? Was this something he did all the time? Hard to understand how a proud woman like you could put up with that kind of betrayal.*

Maxine just sighed and told him that, obviously, she had been fooled. The truth was, she had really thought Albert was loyal to her and never looked at another woman. Now she had been proven wrong. So what? It certainly wasn't the first time that vanity had misled her.

Meeker, his ambitions fueled by "Columbo" reruns, longed to arrest a rich murderess from Schraalenberg. He searched for Albert's other love affairs – and found none. He poured over Maxine's financial situation, only to discover that she had nothing to gain from Albert's murder that she did not possess already. A clear prenuptial arrangement, which she had signed and did not contest, stipulated exactly how she must share his assets with Marcus' widow and the kids.

Faced with a dead end, Meeker committed his files to a disc in a memory, moved on to other cases and started planning his retirement. The aircraft industry stopped obsessing about Albert and got on with its business. Maxine began regularly hiring Marshall, the devoted fan with the navy Mercedes, to take her into the city so she could go out with Ceecee.

Two full years after Albert's death, she felt that it would be appropriate to get back to work on the Frank Dash Garden. A long drought, as anomalous as the rains that had preceded Albert's murder, had delayed the work for yet another season but finally the strange new weather backed off and gave the Garden a pass.

"Time to rock and roll," Maxine said to the contractors.

The Record carried a small article about Maxine's renewed resolve. "Mr. Dash's widow, Maxine Dash Vandeblinken of Schraalenberg, has made a generous grant to the county for the Garden's development and maintenance, which will be matched by the state. Other major sponsors include Monmouth Fine Papers, Keepshape Extrusions, and Teaberg Paints. The Garden is expected to be open to the public in June of next year."

Maxine felt very pleased when the lady from Brights International Express called her and said that the company would be interested in joining the list of businesses supporting Maxine's fine work. She recalled this person from the memorial service for Albert, which she had arranged at the Newark Airport chapel – an attractive young woman of East Indian lineage who was wearing, along with her sari, a pair of tan patent leather Rodriguez Fancy boots. Maxine did have a moment's hesitation. BIX, after all; Albert had a thing about BIX; some old business rivalry. But then she figured, who cares? Albert was dead and money was money, and it would be nice to have at least one corporate sponsor who was not famous for poisoning New Jersey.

Maxine agreed to a lunch. Siloo suggested a place. When Maxine showed up, she found Sam Euphemia.

SHE REALIZED INSTANTLY THAT THIS POKING, probing lunch constituted a kind of forced prepayment for BIX's generosity to the Garden. Not that she was frightened of Euphemia. With his hoarse, rasping voice and bulky eyebrows, he reminded her of an actor she had once known who spent his life playing hit men, henchmen and other heavies. He was no match for her, no matter how attractive those hairy knuckles looked with the gold cufflinks. The violence of his accusation against Albert, however, nearly knocked her off her chair.

"Did you know, Mrs. Vandeblinken, that your husband once made a specialty of selling illegally reconditioned aircraft? He dressed them up to look like new. Fitted them out with bogus parts. Sold them to people who sold them to other people who died when they crashed. Did you know that?"

She was speechless for a moment before summoning back her cool.

"That is certainly a horrible thing to say, Mr. Euphemia. And I cannot imagine that it is true. But say I am a foolish woman, a dope, a dupe, and it is true: what can I possibly do about it? As I have said to all the cops over and over and over again, I had absolutely no knowledge of my husband's business. That was the arrangement between us from the beginning."

Euphemia smiled at her regretfully, as though sympathizing with her pathetic attempt to conceal the truth.

"Do you have a list, Mrs. Vandeblinken? A list of people your husband did business with? People who may have bought or sold his planes or components for them? Brokers, suppliers, agents..."

"Please..." she groaned. "I cannot count the number of times I have been asked that question. The answer is I do not have a list. But if it exists, it must surely be part of the public record."

"We think only part of the list is part of the public record. Maybe there were other people who came to your house..."

"But *everybody* came to our house, Mr. Euphemia. Absolutely everybody. In the early years of our marriage, we had lots of dinner parties for people Albert wanted to cultivate. I think he must have invited everybody in the aviation industry at one time or another. I suspect that would also have included your boss, Mr. Brights."

"Jim was never invited," he said.

"Gee, what an oversight," she quipped sarcastically and immediately regretted it. She softened herself. Sighed. "Listen, I did the food, the flowers, the small talk, but Albert made it clear I should never get friendly with his guests. They were *his* guests, you see. His."

"Didn't that strike you as weird? All that secrecy. Didn't it make you suspicious?"

"No. I didn't care. My marriage gave me a very good life and the ability to do the things I like to do and take care of the people I like to help. That was what I cared about. If my husband had secrets, so be it. Maybe that makes me a callous gold digger in your estimation. But I don't care about your estimation either."

She motioned to the waiter. She had found that preemptively picking up the check was often a good way to humiliate a man at lunch.

"A small plane goes down over the Bay of Fundy," Euphemia said. "The plane had been leased from a company that bought it from another company that had installed some replacement parts from a Swiss company which we are pretty sure had once been owned by your late husband. Three people dead. Okay. A private plane is coming in for a landing at a small airstrip in Connecticut. The engine malfunctions. The plane crashes. Five members of the same family are killed. Examination of the wreckage shows that parts of the engine were much older than other parts. The plane had been acquired originally in a deal brokered by a Canadian who often bought aircraft reconditioned by your husband's company. We can't know if this particular plane was among them because the Canadian is dead. The companies involved are defunct. And there's no receipt no contract no record...

"Try to imagine how we feel at BIX. What if we have unknowingly contracted with such compromised equipment? What if it falls apart with our people inside? On my watch, Mrs. Vandeblinken. *On my watch!*" His face heated up. The hairs of his moustache seemed to bristle and lengthen like the quills of a fighting porcupine. It took all her strength not to push her chair back from the table to escape the fury in his eyes. "I can't allow that," he said.

To Maxine's relief, the waiter came. She slipped her card into his leather folder and gave it right back. Euphemia did not look in the least humiliated.

"The European police don't know for sure who murdered Marcus," he said. "They say drug dealers, but really they've got nothing. Same thing with your husband. Nothing. Is this a family vendetta, Mrs. Vandeblinken? Some Swiss rivalry we don't understand?"

Feeling really uncomfortable now, even a little threatened by the big BIX man, Maxine decided to calm herself by recapturing the chatty babble of a gossip she had once played in a sitcom, and she began telling Sam all kinds of stuff he must already know.

"If there was a history, some feud or something, I wasn't privy," she answered. "Albert's parents were long dead when I met him. His mother is buried in Virginia, oddly enough. I met Marcus for the first time at my wedding. He was maybe 30 at that time. He looked like Albert only taller. He had the family dimples. He wore a beautiful suit and a pale yellow tie that matched his hair, and marvelous gold cufflinks, something like yours, Mr. Euphemia, but not quite so gaudy."

Euphemia appeared to take no offense at her crack. What a tough character he was. Perfectly expressionless. She recalled an acting exercise whose aim was to be perfectly expressionless. Not an easy task.

"Marcus did not bring a date to our wedding, and I remember thinking that because of the elegant way he dressed, he might be gay. Shows you what I know. When he was killed, he left a wife and two children and a mistress who had to be paid off. Her name I can give you, although I imagine she has already been thoroughly investigated.

"Marcus played polo. Albert was very proud of that. He had been quite disadvantaged as a boy, and the ownership of horses seemed to him a sign of prosperity and status. Whenever we went to Europe, we tried to see Marcus play. He and his wife Lin always had us over to their home for dinner. Lin was very nice to me. She's a sophisticated woman from a wealthy family, and I think she took it in stride that Marcus was not faithful to her because she knew he loved her and would never leave her. The kids are wonderful. Paul and Brigitte. Gorgeous in the way that biracial kids often are. They ski, and Paul plays the violin. I hope they will attend American universities, and on holidays they will come to my house, to wash their laundry and eat a good meal." An expression of amused disbelief grazed Euphemia's face. "It seems that the idea of me having a warm relationship with children strikes you as laughable," Maxine said. "You unfeeling son-of-a-bitch."

Apparently hurt to the core, almost in tears, she wiped one eye with the heel of her hand, smearing her mascara, which she had once done very effectively in a daytime soap. Euphemia did not apologize for upsetting her.

As she was getting into the Mercedes, Maxine realized that she had neglected to secure the contribution for the Frank Dash Garden that Euphemia was supposed to have brought to their encounter.

Nuts.

But later that afternoon, a BIX messenger brought her a fragrant gardenia plant and a note – "Thanks for lunch. SE" – clipped to a check for $100,000.

EIGHTEEN.

The Inheritance

IN MARCH, MAXINE DECIDED TO open the vault.

It was cold and quiet. Muir was vacationing at home in Edinburgh. Hannibal had gone to a kennel for grooming and shots.

Maxine sat in her kitchen. Lemon ice lemon ice. She gazed at the blank face of the refrigerator. Albert was dead. All she had to do was go in the vault and get out the stuff she wanted. But she could still hear his soft voice saying "You must never come in here on your own, my darling girl. Never. Am I clear?"

Time to stop being afraid, Maxie, she told herself. Time to claim what is rightfully yours.

She retrieved the key, which she knew Albert had hidden behind one of the tiles around the fireplace, and unlocked his desk. Then she found the magnetic card, which she knew he kept in the false back of the top left drawer. She opened the refrigerator, removed the contents of the top shelf, then the shelf, then she inserted the card and closed the refrigerator. While it was sliding to the side, a wave of excitement swept over her, and like a little kid she thought: "Finally. Finally! Oooh, this is gonna be great, this is gonna be *so great!*" Her heart was pounding, her hands were sweating, her eyes squeezed shut with anticipation.

She opened her eyes. The vault lay shining before her. Except for the red leather sofa, it was empty.

Maxine gave a startled cry. Then she laughed and sighed and shook her head and plopped herself down on the sofa. "Gee honey," she said, "you could at least have left me the turquoise pendant, I mean, just for old time's sake. It would have been so much fun to wear it, once, someplace besides my tired old snatch."

MAXINE DIDN'T KNOW WHAT TO DO. It crossed her mind that she may have *imagined* the treasures of the vault, that they had never really existed, that their presence was just an illusion spun by her sorcerer husband to entrap her and bind her up in her own greed. But of course she knew that wasn't true. All Albert's stuff was real, and he had extracted it in secret to pay some debt or close some deal or reward some girlfriend while she, the dopey, duped widow, waited for it in vain.

"You are such a jerk, Maxie," she said out loud, expecting to feel angry at having been so fooled. But she didn't feel angry, or even very resentful. Actually she felt sort of...light. Even lighthearted. Even relieved.

Leaving the vault door open and all the lights on, she piled into her Jaguar and called Ceecee from the road. "I'm coming to New York. We're going out for pizza. Don't put on any make-up. Let's relax for once."

The great city, ever her beacon, blazed at Maxine as she crossed the river. During a moment when the traffic slowed, she unhooked her bra and pulled it off through the sleeves of her shirt, then tossed it into the back seat. She sang along with Elton John.

Ceecee was waiting on the street in front of her building. She was wearing sneakers. She wore sneakers at every possible opportunity these days, because of the arthritis in her knees.

They went out to a neighborhood joint on the Upper West Side where nobody knew them. Maxine spent the night in the pretty pink room which had previously belonged to Ceecee's daughters and where now their daughters slept during visits to New York. She read their teen magazines and colored in one of their coloring books. Ceecee's dog Crispy slept on her toes for a while before resuming his regular spot by Ceecee's bed.

The next morning she had a facial and a manicure and a pedicure and then, feeling rejuvenated and full of plans – maybe she would start dating again; maybe the happy-go-lucky old Frenchman who owned the perfume company; maybe that nice toy mogul with the scrunched up shoulders; maybe she would order a walk of terracotta stepping stones in the Frank Dash Garden, decorated by the local children, paid for by their parents, in memory of their grandparents - she drove home to Schraalenberg.

The Calder mobile had been installed on the ceiling of the living room.

The two elephants had been placed adjacent to the chairs (Albert's brown leather, hers floral) that girded the fireplace.

The bronze horse and cowboy were set in the center of the dining room table. In the windowed china cabinet, the crystal cash bowls glittered, and all the cash was still in them.

"I will know," Albert had said. "I will always know."

Reaching for the support of the walls, fighting hysteria, Maxine backed up the stairs.

The Hindu goddess had been moved into the bedroom, and all the gold bangles were gathered in her lap. On Maxine's dresser stood the alabaster hand, with the big blue diamond on its fourth finger and the ruby earrings cradled on its palm and the pearls hooked over its thumb. The heavy platinum chain was coiled around the base, the turquoise pendant lying over it like a rattle at the end of a snake.

Frantic, Maxine dug through her closet until she found the 50-year old knife still wrapped in the decaying purple dress with the Hawaii scene on its bosom, which was itself wrapped in a pashmina shawl. Like Ceecee on the desert road, she felt steadier just from holding the awful thing.

She carefully opened the bathroom door, looking for assassins to come lunging at her from the shower. The swan and his nymph now stood next to her tub. Maxine threw up in the toilet.

She washed her face and crept downstairs as far as the third step from the bottom where she collapsed, gripping the knife, exhaling in forceful little blows as she had been taught in a class about alleviating the pain of childbirth. She sat there for a long time, trying to regain control of her body, waiting for the invaders' next move, until finally, she realized that the next move was hers.

OBVIOUSLY, ALBERT HAD LEFT HIS henchmen devilish instructions as to how to deliver the inheritance in case anything ever happened to him. She could just imagine him chuckling as he plotted his scenario. Give it to her, take it away, then let her have it again. How he loved to manipulate her feelings and defeat her with her own desires! Wasn't that one of his favorite games? But now that his little posthumous joke had ended, she was left with the fear that Albert's creepy seconds could be in her house at will and that she was being watched at every moment. Like the cops in Italy and the Hamptons, they could know when she came and went, and if they decided to rob her or kill her, she was helpless against them.

And what if this terrifying redecoration of her home and her ambitions *wasn't* Albert's joke? What if the people who had murdered him had engineered the whole thing, to let her know that if she made the wrong move, she could end up just like the butchered bimbo with the fancy rings?!

How could she escape? Could she sell the house and move west with Ceecee? But what good would that do? If she could be watched here, she could be watched anywhere, and Ceecee with her, and the idea of dragging her precious friend into the viper-filled bed she had made for herself was absolutely unthinkable. She took a deep breath and exhaled. The bestirred Calder turned majestically in her direction.

For a nanosecond she considered calling Detective Meeker and saying, "Look, I am an innocent woman. Tell me if these are stolen goods. If they are, then take them and return them to their rightful owners." But she immediately discarded this idea because after all the self-stifling and feigning and plain old courage that it had taken to stay married to Albert, she sure as hell was not going to abandon the loot that had fallen, no matter by what route, into her lap.

If the stuff was stolen, let someone else finger it.

She decided to go to the gym. Figuring her situation from every angle over and over, she walked the treadmill until she felt faint, and the young girls there insisted that she must sit down and rest. She stopped at a delicatessen and bought a filet of herring in cream sauce and stood in the street and ate the whole thing, every last crystallized onion and sour sweet smear. She watched a night of television, clicking and clicking and thinking and thinking, and fell asleep with the set still babbling. And the next morning when she woke, she knew that she was trapped. There was no way out.

Returning from Scotland, Muir inquired whether Madam had any particular cleaning instructions pertaining to the new objects in the house, with their ebony and ivory and gold embossed leather and such.

"You know I have nothing to impart about cleaning, Muir," snapped Maxine. "That's a foolish question. Go consult some expert. Call Marian and Mint, the antique people. Just do it."

"And the flying sculpture, Mrs. Vandeblinken? It's rather dirty."

"Let it be dirty."

"But that is against my nature, Madam."

"I do not give a damn about your nature, Muir, now get the hell off my back!"

Biting back tears, Muir withdrew. Maxine felt terrible, and she hated Muir, all the more so since Muir could have no idea how dirty the Calder actually was. "Damn you, Albert," she whispered, as she knocked on Muir's door, compelled to apologize for her nastiness.

MAXINE COMMENCED TO THROW HERSELF into a burgeoning public life as the most elegant and generous benefactress in the Garden State, for she had now determined that since Albert's successors had provided her with the necessary sets and costumes, this was to be her new soap opera and, she thought wryly, probably her last role. She began to integrate the vault treasures into her appearances, secretly hoping that if she showed them off, somebody might be roused to steal them or pronounce them stolen and repossess them.

To give herself the right backdrop against which to display the ruby earrings, she ordered a spectacular gown from Mr. Zapata in Paris. A vast red taffeta creation with long, tight-fitting sleeves and a snug bodice studded with Chinese coins, the dress refused to expand until it reached the hip, and then it suddenly rolled out in yards of bustles and ruffles, tumultuous as the Red Sea during the crossing. Maxine intended to wear it to the benefit for the Native American Scholarship Fund, to which she had made a large contribution. She wanted to make a splash there, as the Red Sea had done.

Unlike other women of her type, Maxine wore only one gown in a season. To sport a different outfit for each charitable affair seemed to her a waste of money, which might otherwise be given to the charity itself. She planned to wear the dress to the formal ball benefiting the clean-up of the Hackensack River, at the annual music industry honors which she was attending with one of her old lovers who would be receiving (alas!) a Lifetime Achievement Award, and at the opening of a new museum dedicated to fiber arts, one of Ceecee's pet philanthropies.

Seven times at least she would wear the grand taffeta gown before tucking it away into storage. Seven times she would have to force herself to wear the ruby earrings, even though she felt haunted by the sensation that each precious stone had a tiny little recording device implanted in it that reported her every word to phantom eavesdroppers.

She wore some of the gold bangles to the gala for the Humane Society. They bumped against each other with a delicate chime. She imagined that people were staring at them, as though they were tell-tale links left over after an escape from the chain gang. She wore the pearls to the dinner for the Sisters of Mercy Hospice, suspecting all the while that the diamond clasp was broadcasting her heart's truth to heaven.

For the opening of the Frank Dash Garden in June, she wore the big blue diamond ring. Public doubt about its authenticity, *her* authenticity, made it feel like a hunk of lead on her finger, all the more so since that damn glowering BIX man, who should have been far away at his home office in California, decided to make a surprise appearance.

NINETEEN.
Humanized Nature

FEDERAL PARK WAS SET HIGH above the Hudson River, across from New York, not far from Schraalenberg, near the ruins of an old Civilian Conservation Corps encampment from the '30s. You could reach it by turning off the Palisades Parkway onto a winding road with speed bumps. The road led you to a gravel lot where you could leave your car. Then you continued on foot down a pine needle path, which led you to a sign that said you were now entering The Frank Dash Memorial Garden.

As the representative of a major corporate donor, Sam was welcomed with a certain amount of genuflection. Stewards wearing T-shirts imprinted with Frank Dash landscape photos escorted him across a stone bridge, through a grove of young spruces being trained into an arbor, and onto a mossy field to a party with several hundred guests and a jazz combo and waiters offering champagne in plastic glasses.

Authentic nature lovers, those who had battled the developers and lobbied ceaselessly on behalf of the Garden, the carriers of signs, circulators of petitions, stuffers of envelopes, mingled with the CEOs and the rich philanthropists. They were the happiest people present. Clear conscience; job well done. They drank the most and stayed the longest and beamed most brightly.

The party crawled with politicians.

Sam allowed himself to be photographed with one of them who

had been helpful to BIX on a tariff matter. Someone brought him a glass of wine. He tipped the glass toward a good looking waitress who had been trying her best to get his attention. Shook hands with an airport executive who introduced him to a jolly fat guy who owned warehouses out on Route 3. This man had a gripe with FedEx and was thinking about changing couriers. Sam texted Siloo and asked her to set up a meeting.

He scanned the party for Maxine. Couldn't find her. Then he realized she was right up there at the podium, wearing a silver dress and a gigantic diamond ring, and she was making a speech.

"Maybe because from an early age he was misshapen himself," Maxine told the crowd, "Frank Dash was all the more appreciative of what a miracle beauty was, what a fantastic gift of nature."

What did she mean, misshapen? Sam had been so engaged in his own entrance to this party that he had not looked closely at the booklet about Frank Dash, which had been distributed to everyone. There on the cover was the famous photographer. Big head, twisted back, big torso, short legs, big camera, big smile. Maxine's first husband had been a little person! Amazing! Sam had heard it said that men of genius often attracted knockout women regardless of their own personal appearance, but he had never believed it until now.

Maxine spoke of Frank's fascination with the forms and hues of growing, living things; of his friendships with other great artists, people like Ansel Adams and Alexander Calder; of his devotion to the community. "Every day, Frank would take his motorized bike with the side car that held his camera and his tripods, and he would ride into Central Park to take pictures of dogs playing with people. 'The dogs remind us of our innocence,' he used to say. 'They remind us of the love we experienced when we were very young, before pain, before abandonment and betrayal, before any kind of public destiny invaded our little lives.'

"Dogs with people. People with flowers. Those were the formulas of Frank Dash, his medicines for what ailed him, for what ails us. So in keeping with Frank's philosophy, this park has a garden path for everyone, including the wheelchair bound and the blind. And you will also find here several fenced acres where the dogs we love may be unleashed and allowed to run and play in freedom.

"On behalf of all the wonderful corporate sponsors and government partners and committed individuals who funded and solicited the funding for everything you see here today, I am honored to welcome you to this monument to Frank's lifetime dedications: the development of nature photography, the advancement of an idea of natural beauty which is, above all, friendly to people."

The crowd applauded heartily. Sam hissed from behind his teeth and shook his head at the irony of it. They liked her. They actually thought she was a nice woman.

A short guy appeared suddenly like a leprechaun popping out from under a mushroom and grabbed Sam's sleeve. "Hey Samster, what a surprise!" Big smile; shaved bald; sweaty; who the hell was he? "Shit, look at you with your cufflinks! Good to see you're back in the neighborhood. Heard you were a big shot in the delivery business. Heard your mom got married again. Heard she's renting out the house on Rumble Street."

Sam squinted at him. "And you are…"

"Charlie Fleeger, you forgot me, hell, we're not that old, we were friends, I thought, back in the day, we were really good friends, well, but anyway it's okay, I'm the mayor of Pettyboro now, here's my card, take care."

And trying not to show how devastated he was to have been forgotten, Charlie scurried away.

So many goddamned people. Such a pile up of people, even well and closely known in eras lost to memory. Why did others remember him while he forgot them? So what if he was busy; was he so much busier than everybody else? Had his memory melted completely and forever in the South American prison? Was it physical? Early onset of a dread mental deterioration? Maybe something that ran in his father's family, those disappeared Italians with their buried genetic codes.

Shasta Nakamura said "Hi." Then again. *Sam. Hi.*

He found it difficult to look at her. Ashamed of his condition, he had not called her since his return, and now he was ashamed about that too. She was holding her eight-year old son's hand and carrying her four-year old daughter. She was wearing a pale green dress. Her bare arms spoke to him, recalling to him their strength. All the world's races seemed to be mixed together in her children. As Maxine had said of Marcus and Lin Vandeblinken's kids: gorgeous.

"How uh how… how do you come to be here?" he asked.

"Rodriguez Fancy. My biggest customer. They stayed with us after the orchid mess. We couldn't have recovered without them. We bring their boots in from the workshop in Arizona almost every day and ship them everywhere." She grinned and kicked out her foot to show him her boots.

He took her hand. Started to mumble some explanation.

She shook her head, making the explanation unnecessary.

She led him into a group of Spanish speakers and introduced him to Ceecee Blochner and her daughters. Sam tried hard to plant their names and traits in his mind as he had done so handily in his old life. Gladdy, the VP for sales, big brown eyes, big tits, blue boots. Rosie, the CFO, glasses, big tits, red boots. They were joined by Assemblyman George Arroyo. Handsome; short; not as short as Charlie Fleeger. *Oh Jesus, how could he have forgotten Charlie?!*

Assemblyman Arroyo underscored the exclusivity of his friendship with the Blochners by injecting witty side remarks in Spanish. But Sam knew Spanish. And he was much taller than the Assemblyman. And his suit was ten times as expensive.

"I'm familiar with your record, sir," Sam said. "You represent my hometown. Pettyboro."

"I'll bet you don't live there anymore," Arroyo joked.

"That's right."

"What intelligent person would? Miserable little town. Just miserable. Dark and depressed."

"Still its citizens manage to hang on," Sam growled.

Someone else might have heeded the warning in his tone. However,

Arroyo was one of those less than gifted politicians who could not listen and speak at the same time.

"I went to Pettyboro once to make a speech at the high school," he continued. "Let me tell you, that was some bizarre experience. Every five minutes or so, there was this rumbling sound and a kind of creepy shaking, like the whole building was about to collapse. Scar-ree. Some towns have no reason to be towns. No economy. No business. Pettyboro is like that. A big garbage dump with a municipal designation. When I talked with the kids afterwards, you can bet, all of them, let me tell you, every single one of them had plans to get out."

"No one ever gets out of Pettyboro," Sam said. "Even after you leave, you're still there."

Maxine Vandeblinken joined the group. She expected to be greeted with hugs and compliments for her presentation, but at that particular moment, no one in her fan club wanted to interrupt Sam.

"We don't forget the explosion," he was saying. "It was a long time ago. But we got plaques all over to remind us. Did you notice the plaques when you made your speech, Assemblyman?"

The politician finally woke up to the fact that his rant about garbage dumps had not been well received.

"I didn't mean to appear insensitive."

"That's exactly how you appeared."

"Then I sincerely apologize."

"What explosion?" Maxine asked.

Arroyo could have choked her.

Shasta's little boy suddenly reached into the grass and picked up a lady bug and held it out to his sister on the pad of his index finger. The child laughed as the lady bug crossed over into her palm.

"A bad story," Sam said. "Not appropriate to tell in such innocent company."

But he couldn't get out of it. The eyes of all the women, so intent and interested, the wounding of his old pal Charlie, the adorable kids encircled by their mother's arms, all of it softened the steel inside Sam Euphemia, and he could not help but tell.

"Okay, so the ground is packed with garbage," he explained. "It's fermenting down there for years. Nobody pays any attention. Nobody tells the people. Then, one day, the place just blows. My dad Angelo Euphemia was working with his crew on a sewer line. The explosion opened up a crater, and it swallowed them. Some of the pieces of those men are still buried in Garbage Mountain. I was eight.

"It gets called an accident. But you feel all your life like it was really just plain murder. So all your life you want somebody to hang for it. The Mob, the chemical companies, you'll excuse me, Mr. Arroyo, the politicians. But nobody ever does. That's what makes Pettyboro such a depressed little town, Assemblyman. Not enough justice."

In a few moments with Maxine Vandeblinken and her friends, Sam had revealed more about himself than ever before at a public occasion. He became self-conscious. He wiped his sun glasses with the immaculate white linen handkerchief he always kept in his breast pocket.

"What Pettyboro really needs is for someone to build a garden like this on Garbage Mountain," he said. "Then maybe the rumbling and the shaking would stop. And in time, nobody would remember that it was all refuse and dead bodies underneath, and people could go there to have picnics and look out at the ships in the harbor and count the planes flying over."

TWENTY.

On Garbage Mountain

ALL HER FRANTIC PHILANTHROPY HAD not served to placate the uneasiness Maxine had been feeling ever since her lunch with Sam Euphemia. He obviously represented not just his own but a whole body of opinion about her late husband. She had not been able to amuse him or embarrass him or change the subject. He had not believed her when she said she knew nothing, otherwise he would never have sent the check. That fucking check was his permission slip to go on probing and poking without cease.

She had tried to laugh off Sam's relentless hostility in her post mortems with Ceecee. *A minor executive whose suit outclasses him. His vocal disability makes his every word sound like a warning shot.* But then Euphemia showed up at the Garden opening and told that story about the sanitary landfill and everything changed. Ceecee and her daughters and their courier, an entrepreneurial woman for whom Maxine had a lot of respect, actually seemed to like him.

This unsettling irony pricked at her mind all through the remainder of the Garden's great opening day. On her way home in the navy Mercedes, when she saw the exit for Pettyboro just under the flight path of the incoming planes, she said: "Turn here, Marshall, please."

They set forth upon a two lane road sporadically lined by bunker-like stores selling tires, machine parts, lumber, plumbing supplies, breakfast. Marshall's eyes sought hers in the rear view mirror.

"Where are we going?"

Maxine flapped her hand several times in a gesture that said "Onward." The road narrowed. The bunkers ended. On both sides of the road, a sea of reeds closed in. Every once in a while, some wrecked thing protruded from among them: a rusted car, trunk gaping; a snow plow upended, gulls on its blade; a rutted chunk of concrete.

Some trash trucks passed the Mercedes, sending forth a nauseating stench. Marshall closed the windows and turned on the air. He followed the trucks up a hill, then onto a black iron bridge that clashed and clanged under the wheels. Exiting the bridge, they came face to face with Garbage Mountain. It rose up from the devastated wetland that stretched for miles all around them, a flattop monolith capped in patches of steam, spotted with splotches of unnatural neon color. Access roads cut into its sides. Trucks crawled toward the summit to drop their loads, then raced down.

Marshall stopped the car and turned around to face Maxine.

"Are we lost?"

"No. Go on. Let's see more."

They drove straight on. They passed through the town of Pettyboro. They saw an old soldier's park, two gas stations, a steakhouse with a neon sign that flashed *Mary's M ry's*, a bank, a school, probably the high school where Arroyo had made his speech. In the distance to the left, they noted a large concrete building with barred windows, a high cyclone fence and its own gated approach road.

"Looks like an asylum, or a penitentiary," Marshall offered.

Garbage Mountain was so close now that it blocked the view. Nothing west of it could be seen, and very soon, nothing north or south. The gulls, in herds of thousands, darkened the sky and made a deafening noise. The Mercedes seemed to enter the Mountain's embrace. Marshall repeatedly checked the road behind, to reassure himself that there was still a way out.

They entered an area of narrow houses squashed against each other on short streets. Some of the houses were painted in bold colors. Some no longer even tried. The street names – Shiver, Rocking, Jumpy,

Rumble – described what life was like in the shadow of the landfill. At Maxine's direction, Marshall drove very slowly among them, past the funeral home, the VFW hall, two or three bars, a large, plain church. They experienced the shaking which Arroyo had spoken of, as the compacted trash all around them shifted and swelled and writhed in its own gases.

In the few minutes it took Maxine to tour Pettyboro, dozens of people abandoned their work to observe her. Jackhammers stopped hammering. Window washers hung suspended, their squeegees stilled. Clerks walked out from behind their counters and stood in the doorways with their customers, watching. Eleanor Euphemia's tenant and her neighbor stopped gossiping on the concrete stoop of the house on Rumble Street to stare and wonder.

Marshall drove past them and continued on the road up Garbage Mountain. He drove as far as possible and then stopped. Despite his protests, Maxine got out of the car and, in her high heels, continued alone on foot.

The grave of everything stretched out before her. The birds swarmed over it, like flies over manure. Not one green fleck of nature's mercy brightened the day. Yet Maxine threw back her head and laughed and clapped her hands with glee. For she had suddenly realized, standing among the horrors of Garbage Mountain, that with a little finesse and some money, she could banish all her enemies in this place, and their power would lie squashed under the gull poop among the bones of other gangsters, helpless to harm her or anyone she cared about forever more.

DURING THE ENSUING WEEKS, Maxine brought experts to her bank to appraise the gems in her safe deposit box, and then to Fifteen Willow Cascade to evaluate some of the artworks there. She lounged in her flowered chair, her feet up on the ottoman, while the appraisers moved silkily among her possessions. Not one asked about the Calder or raised any suspicion about its past.

She invited Detective Meeker to lunch.

He had long ago given up trying to make a case against her. In just a few months, he would retire. Various excellent security jobs awaited him. However, this invitation raised anew his hopes for one final crack at celebrity. He took a barber shop shave and wore a wire.

It was a lovely day in the early fall. Maxine's garden was bursting with tomatoes and yellow crookneck squash and chrysanthemums. Muir served a lunch of rolled roast beef sandwiches with horse radish sauce for dipping and salad and apple pie and coffee. Maxine chatted amiably, questioning Meeker about his own family and his plans for the future, and then took him for a walk through the house and around the grounds. There were witnesses everywhere. A young woman polishing a statue. A handyman on a ladder re-grouting bricks. Gardeners mowing, deadheading, hoeing the beds.

Maxine put her arm on Meeker's, not like an attractive woman seeking to flirt but like an older lady, seeking safe passage. Her dog Hannibal loped on ahead of them. Maxine threw him his favorite toy to chase. To her consternation, he had a hard time seeing where it had landed. Was he losing his sight? Developing cataracts?

She would have to call the vet.

She pointed to this rare breed of hydrangea and that froth of autumn clematis, never letting go of Meeker. "So tell me, Detective, did you notice anything funny about the house? Look at the mums."

"There is so much surveillance equipment in your house, Mrs. Vandeblinken," Meeker answered "that it reminds me of a military installation."

"Maxine. Maxine. Please. Maxine. Look at the tomatoes. There is a deep cave, a kind of vault, behind the refrigerator. I could show you how to get in there. Some tiles on the shower ceiling seem slightly askew. I think recording devices may be hiding behind them. I'm sure there's more to be found."

"Why did you invite me here, Mrs. Va...Maxine?"

"Because I have only recently become aware of how thoroughly the house is bugged. And it's making me crazy. Look at the roses. Admire the bird house. I have the feeling that I am being watched all the time..."

"Well, you sure are."

"I feel that my phone calls are being listened to..."

"Your husband must have had a lot to fear."

"Perhaps he did. But you see, Detective, I do not. I have nothing to hide and nothing to fear. And now that you've come here and corroborated my suspicions, that there's all this listening and watching equipment all over the house, I was hoping, I mean since you're retiring and you may be looking for additional jobs that utilize your skills and your connections, that maybe you could help me have it all removed. Here, take some zucchini." She began to fill a basket. The vegetables were warm from the sun.

"Sure, I could," Meeker offered. "But you would have to give letters, with your permission, official permission, and there would be reports and local law enforcement would know everything, and I mean everything about your house."

Maxine laughed bitterly. "My house? Are you kidding? Please... Listen, Detective. I am going to California in two weeks to attend a benefit for the Getty Museum, and after that, I'm going on to a spa in Baja to rest my mind. During that time, I want you to get rid of it all. Bring a wire person to tear out the wires, a camera person to take out the cameras, bring the FBI and the FAA and the CIA for all I care. I'll write whatever letters you require. I'll arrange with Muir to let you in. She'll give you and your people every assistance. I will pay whatever is necessary. If it's not illegal or immoral or any kind of a conflict with any other commitment you may have, you can add 20% as a fee for yourself, for supervising. And then, when it's all done, and the cameras and the listening devices are gone..." she placed the brimming basket in Meeker's capable hands "...*then*, it will be my house."

ARMED WITH THE CERTIFICATES OF APPRAISAL, Maxine arranged several meetings with her accountant. She took a day trip to Trenton to have lunch with Assemblyman Arroyo and some key leaders in the State Legislature. She arranged a dinner in New Brunswick with a professor who was an old lover of Ceecee's and a good friend of the governor. Finally she called the BIX office near Newark Airport where Sam Euphemia and his staff had now settled. She left a message with Siloo to the effect that upon her return from California, she was scheduling an exploratory trip with Assemblyman Arroyo up to Garbage Mountain, to plan her next garden. Since this new project had been conceived at Mr. Euphemia's suggestion, she hoped he would join the expedition.

Maxine sat on the arm of the red sofa in the vault that evening and spoke aloud to what she now believed to be the vast, all-seeing organization which had moved in with her after Albert's death.

"I have two things to tell you, whoever you are," she said. "First. The police have detected lots of surveillance equipment here and that has made them very suspicious and given them an excuse to snoop, so I have agreed to let them take it out, really, I had no choice. Sorry, fellas. Second. I need money for a new charitable project. So I've decided to sell some of the jewels and works of art which I recently received from Mr. Vandeblinken's estate. I'm going to use the proceeds to endow the state of New Jersey with a large matching grant to launch the building of a new park on Garbage Mountain. Seems to me a fitting thing for Albert Vandeblinken's widow to do, to take a dreadful ugly eyesore and turn it into a ravishing garden, since I've recently heard that Albert himself was such an expert at beautifying broken old things.

"With the permission of the authorities, which will certainly be granted, I am going to call it The Albert Vandeblinken Memorial Garden. I feel sure that Albert would be pleased."

Before she left for California, Maxine filed all the necessary papers with Detective Meeker and gave him the magnetic card that opened the vault. He and his people came into Fifteen Willow Cascade while she was away and stripped the house of its many eyes and ears. If they left other eyes and ears in their place, well, who cares, she thought. As long as you had to be watched, you might as well be watched by cops of your own choosing.

part

———

7

TWENTY-ONE.

Gumpy

FOR THE EXPLORATORY TRIP TO Garbage Mountain, Maxine picked up Assemblyman Arroyo at his office. Having heard that the intimidating Sam Euphemia of BIX would be along for this ride, Arroyo wore his new blue suede blazer. He felt disappointed that Euphemia arrived separately, in his own Subaru, wearing jeans and a sweatshirt, needing a shave. Then a seagull bombed Assemblyman Arroyo, leaving upon his beautiful jacket a long brown and white stain that would never come out.

The smell of the landfill was sickening. The men covered their noses and gagged. Not Maxine. When a bulldozer came along, churning the garbage, she climbed on board, dragging Arroyo with her, and took off across the festering plain, flattering the driver with eager questions. Sam stayed behind. He kicked at the gravel road like a disgruntled teenager.

The driver said that the whole area had once been owned by a crazy millionaire who built a mansion in the middle of it and took his guests on fishing trips and bird watching outings among the reeds and maintained really beautiful gardens. When he needed cash in the Depression, the millionaire sold eighty acres to a pig farmer, who opened a dump and fed his pigs on garbage. The millionaire kept on losing money. He decided to sell his mansion. Nobody would buy it because nobody wanted to live next to the pigs and the dump. It stood abandoned, filled with homeless squatters, until someone burned it down.

The pig farmer closed the dump in the 50s, when it became illegal to sell refuse-fed pork to the public. After a while, the Mob, which had run trash collection in the Garden State until relatively recently, reopened it, but "sort of informally", the bulldozer driver joked, and what was buried there during those years remained a secret.

In the imagination of the people, the ever-growing landfill seemed to brew perpetual life-in-death. Malevolent ghosts of murdered murderers rose from the garbage to incite bloody vendettas that in turn brought new corpses for burial. Some plants and animals that had once thrived near the landfill starved and died out. Others grew to unprecedented numbers, un-thinned by their regular enemies, who had somehow disappeared.

Arroyo controlled his rising gorge until they arrived back at the gravel road. Then he vomited as discreetly as possible behind a stack of bald tires. Sam gave him a bottle of water and a towel and said: "Mrs. Vandeblinken, it looks like you don't mind the stink of corruption. So if you want to stick around here, go right ahead. If you really think you can turn Garbage Mountain into a garden spot, BIX will consider a contribution. But right now, I'm taking Assemblyman Arroyo back to Trenton."

ARROYO HAD HOPED, AFTER THAT MORNING, never to have to deal with Garbage Mountain again. However, driven by Maxine's generosity to his campaign for the State Senate and a vague feeling that her crazy project might turn out not to be so crazy, he got some funds inserted into New Jersey's budget to research the idea of creating a garden in the horrible place.

The press dubbed the Garbage Mountain Project "GUMPY", a cynical cross between "dump" and "gimp", since it was assumed that the project had been born crippled and was doomed to fail. Administration of GUMPY fell to the Environmental Sciences Department at the University of New Jersey in the Pine Barrens, popularly known as "PB." The man in charge was Professor Ivan Binkley.

Binkley taught Forestry. He had been named supervisor of

GUMPY, even though he was only an Associate, because no one more qualified had the stomach for the fieldwork. He was a midsized, muscular, nearsighted West Virginian with floppy gray-and-brown hair and calloused hands that displayed a fantastic array of injuries. One middle finger appeared to have five joints from having been broken so often. An angry turtle had snapped off the tip of his left thumb. Permanent chemical discolorations streaked both palms.

Binkley's Garbage Mountain Regeneration Team, known as "the Gumrats", included a botanist, a soil chemist, a plant pathologist, two solid waste disposal experts and six grad students from PB. Maxine loved hanging with this gang. Like Ceecee, the Gumrats were gifted people who had to be protected, and Maxine knew how to do that. She felt competent and respected among them, and because of the peculiar nature of their work, righteous too. Now that was certainly a nice new feeling.

Sam Euphemia stayed aloof from the project even though he represented GUMPY's biggest corporate sponsor and as such was the most powerful member of the Board. Here they were, right on the fringes of his home town, and he hardly ever visited. Maybe his little outburst at the Frank Dash Garden was less sincere than she had perceived. Maybe he cared less than he seemed to. Or maybe he cared much more than he would ever let on.

"What is he hiding?" she asked Shasta Nakamura, Ceecee's courier who seemed to like Sam, might even (Ceecee thought this) be sleeping with him.

Shasta answered "He is hiding his whole heart and soul!" and tears spurted onto her lashes.

Maxine backed off quickly, for this was much more of an answer than she had cared to receive.

Euphemia did see to it that Shasta's spin-off company, Flora Shipments International, known as FSI, scored the contract to handle GUMPY's transport management. Shasta bought a couple of used vans and had them painted green.

MAXINE IMAGINED THAT, AS soon as GUMPY had completed its research and decided on a landscape plan, the dump would be closed, that Garbage Mountain would be leveled off, smoothed over, and covered with a pretty deciduous forest whose roots would hold down the trash and prevent erosion and whose fallen leaves would rot and create deeper soil with each successive season, the better to plant cascading beds of purple and pink azaleas that would dazzle passing drivers on the Turnpike and rehabilitate the image of the Garden State.

In a pasta place near the Trenton train station, Professor Binkley tried to disabuse her of this fantasy.

"The trouble is, Mrs. V, you can't just bury garbage," he said. "If you do, it might possibly poison the soil and the water. And there's a real good chance it might possibly make itself into some dangerous gas and then explode."

First, he explained, gigantic cells had to be excavated to contain the garbage. Then the cells would be lined with bedrock, then three feet of clay, then huge plastic earth diapers that would prevent moisture leakage, then geosynthetic materials to trap water (which would be pumped out and piped to a purification plant), then a layer of sand, then a five-foot layer of degradable paper. Only then, Binkley concluded, might it be possible to dump the accumulated tons of garbage on top.

As this lecture on encapsulation progressed, Maxine, groaning softly, slowly sank onto the table in a parody of exhaustion. Never one to get a joke too quickly, Binkley thought the eccentric rich lady might possibly just be resting. So he continued with his explanation.

"Then when the cell is just about filled," he went on, "a permanent cap may be laid down over it. On top of that you'd need two feet of gravel, maybe three feet of clay, then a geo-composite layer to drain water, then another impervious natural container layer. I've heard tell they make them out of pulverized soda bottles now. And then on top, tons and tons of clean soil, four to six feet deep. My guess is that just might turn out to be the single most expensive part."

In a small voice from among the forks and knives and napkins, Maxine called: "*Now* can we plant an azalea?"

"Well, it's not real advisable since there would be pipes sticking up all over to let the gas escape into traps so it can be purified for use in local institutions. Woody understory plants like azaleas might impede access to the gas. So most people would most likely plant grass."

"Grass?!"

"Yes ma'am. Plain green grass. Actually this might possibly turn out to be real convenient for us here in Jersey because Rutgers has a particular expertise in turf."

"But surely there must be something else!"

"Well I've heard tell about successful cases of phytoremediation, most especially with poplars and sycamores. But those dumps are in different climates, with different pollutants than our GUMPY." He sighed. "We can clean it up, Mrs. V. But I sure don't know if we can ever make it real pretty."

Maxine raised herself from the table top, smoothing her mussed hair and repositioning one of her earrings.

"You know what I think, Professor; may I call you Ivan? I think what we need is a training farm."

"Excuse me?"

"A training farm, like the one my Aunt Gladdy built to teach us how to cope with the new world order."

"Ma'am?"

"Nothing huge or fancy. Just a simple little patch of our own Garbage Mountain, where we can experiment with this plant and that tree and we can see: who has the strength to adapt and who would rather die than grow up in a sanitary landfill."

Binkley took a sip of his tea, looked at her, shut his eyes tightly, looked at her again, took another sip of tea. "That," he said, "may just be a real good idea."

IT WAS DECIDED THAT 12 ACRES on the north side of Garbage Mountain, known thereafter as "the N12", would be taken out of operation as a dumping ground and reserved for experiments in horticultural adaptation. To compensate the dump's owners and the town of

Pettyboro for the lost revenue, GUMPY paid a very generous rent.

At the highest point of the N12 stood the Toxic Greenhouse Experimental Laboratory (called "TOXY" by the Gumrats from PB who did all the filthy grunt labor), where the plants were grown in pots of Garbage Mountain itself and Binkley's cameras and computers and delicate measuring devices worked 24-7. Nobody could enter TOXY without a security clearance and special protective clothing. You had to shower before they would let you out.

The Gumrats gathered at TOXY every morning at seven and then fanned out across the N12, wrapped in yellow plastic ponchos, gauntlets, moon boots and masks. They slogged through leachate puddles made azure and cerise by chemical waste. They snagged their pants on protruding legs of lawn chairs and Christmas tree ornaments which had been discarded in the 70s. They did autopsies on captured bugs.

Maxine visited GUMPY every Thursday, right before her massage. Of course, she wore one of Mr. Zapata's North Coast slickers and his famous thigh-high Gloucester fisherman boots to keep from getting dirty. But she always strode unmasked across the N12, the smell of the training farm disturbing her not at all.

The Gumrats were crazy about her.

She made encouraging speeches to the kids as they tested the fizzing soil samples and sat blinking blearily at the computer screens. To inspire them, she trotted out photos of luxuriant Olmstead landscapes from North Carolina and Massachusetts, the embroidered gardens of the Veneto, the rose fields of Oregon. She brought candy bars to give the Gumrats strength, as well as crates of a miraculous deodorant soap called Lemonish.

Shasta Nakamura's FSI couriers flew all over the country on BIX planes, picking up samples of plants successful in other landfills, filling out endless forms to comply with USDA regulations, collecting and carefully packaging shoots and saplings that might, just might, take hold on Garbage Mountain. The Gumrats planted hardy oaks, birches, beeches, willows, cedars and every kind of maple. They all died.

"Never give up!" Maxine said to the downhearted kids, doing Churchill.

"Nevah nevah nevah nevahnevahnevah!" She installed a sound system that played their favorite music so that, when they needed to, they could dance.

In an act of desperation bordering on the illegal, Binkley ordered two flats of a creeping vine from Georgia that had been known to swallow whole counties. Shasta went personally with her driver to collect the vine from the lab in Decatur, which had been set up specifically to eradicate the voracious thing. During the trip home, she called Binkley from Virginia to report that already little green tendrils were creeping out of the crates in her van, reaching toward the damp air of New Jersey with hydroponic zeal.

The Gumrats planted the shoots immediately upon their arrival. They died overnight.

All of GUMPY was feeling very blue. Maxine couldn't stand that. The next morning, she arrived in an FSI van carrying an easily assembled basketball apparatus. From then on, whenever a breeze blessed their project with a relatively unscented hour, the GUMPY crew shot some hoops at what became known as "Maxie's Rim." Maxine and Marshall came to many of the games with Hannibal, GUMPY's beloved mascot, and leaned on the Mercedes and cheered.

It was more fun than anything Maxine had done in years. She felt young, she felt loved and respected. Her public image, neglected for so long because of Albert's pathological need for privacy, resurfaced. All the newspapers were writing about the encapsulation of the landfill at Garbage Mountain. TV crews hiked out to take pictures. Publicity – so expensive in days gone by – now rolled in like a river, for free. Maxine's face was everywhere. The media heaped praise upon her. They called her The Garden Lady. In the gym and the beauty parlor, perfect strangers shook her hand and thanked her for her public-spirited generosity. And then Sam Euphemia would show up like a bad review.

Maxine's strategy with him, pioneered by the government during the recent wars, had been to embed him more and more deeply into GUMPY's affairs, expecting that the closer he came, the more likely he might be to lose sight of his original objective, which was to link her to the bygone shenanigans of her dead husband. The strategy didn't work. No strategy had ever worked with Sam. He would wait on the outskirts of the N12 until she was ready to leave and then press into her hand a list.

Peru, 1996. A rented four-seater goes down in the Andes. Pilot had reported engine trouble. Everyone lost. Bogus parts suspected. New Mexico, 1997. Private jet makes an emergency landing in the desert. Pilot had reported engine trouble. Bogus parts suspected. Everybody survives. Investigation ongoing.

A month later, he would bring another list. *Tuscany. 1998. Denmark. Oklahoma.* And six weeks after that: *Vermont.*

"Oh, come on, give me a break, Sam. How often must I tell you..."

He cut her off. "We're beginning to see patterns," he said. "The FBI is beginning to think this isn't a random plane-by-plane operation, but a real manufacturing set-up, like with factories and warehouses and distribution. And investors."

TWENTY-TWO.

Reclining Women

IVAN BINKLEY HAD A LABOR shortage. He pressed Sam to seek help from his old friend, Charlie Fleeger. Sam didn't want to. But he had started to feel a little sentimental about GUMPY, the enormity of it, the impossibility of it, the dusty, sweaty, overworked kids. In recent weeks, he had even joined in to play an occasional game with them, crouching like a lion under "Maxie's Rim" and leaping at the last moment to foil the incoming layups. Despite his reluctance to face Charlie, Sam said okay.

He found Mayor Fleeger sitting like a king in his office. He wore a plaid vest and a black shirt, a tweed jacket and a black tie. Trophies and awards girded him. Photos of his wife and four cute kids were installed on the wall above a large plaque from Zonta, honoring him for his contributions to the cause of women's health. His desk, a gigantic relic, lay before him like a captive nation. On its outermost edge, a big bowl of cherry tomatoes proclaimed: "This is the fruit of New Jersey. Help yourself!"

As the leader of Pettyboro, Charlie was pledged to improve the town, to tempt new businesses to set up shop there, providing new jobs. So far, the only business he had managed to attract was a big jail, a kind of safety net for felons who were doing time for lesser offenses and had some prayer of rehabilitation if only they could be kept out of the state penitentiary.

"Hey old buddy, glad to see you got your memory back," he said nastily. "How's your Mom?"

"She's okay."

"You like the new guy?"

"I didn't come here to chitchat, Charlie."

The Mayor lost it.

"Why not?! What the fuck is wrong with you?! Why the hell can't you participate in a coupla minutes of catching up with somebody who used to be your best fucking friend in the world?! How about asking *me* who I married, what kinda kids *I* got, how's *my* mother who fed you in her kitchen maybe a thousand times?! What the hell happened to you?! You used to be a human being."

Sam started to apologize. He really did. It would have been a defining moment, a sign of recovery. But before he could get out the words, Charlie said "Ah fuck it. I don't give a shit. Waddya want?"

"You know this garden, the Vandeblinken Memorial Garden that's getting built on Garbage Mountain..."

"Am I supposed to believe there's really gonna be a garden?"

"Next month, our courier is bringing up six trucks full of irises, more than 4000. Somebody has to plant them. What do we have to do to get the guys from the prison to help out?"

"Are they gonna die from this job?"

"No. But they may puke from the smell. We'll give them masks and gloves and boots and rubber coveralls. What do we have to do?"

"You gotta pay," said Charlie.

"How much?"

Charlie named an exceptionally high figure. His old friend, although burdened by guilt, still didn't feel bad enough to accept such unfavorable terms and agreed to pay one third. For Pettyboro, it was a terrific deal.

Originally from the swamps of the world, haphazardly colored in golds and purples, the irises had been technicolored during their years among humans. Some of them had been bred to turn baby pink and robins' egg blue. The labial falls that hung beneath each blossom had been re-trained to contrast; wine with the pink, white with the blue. But the machinery of the flower still did its work. The gooey pathways with their high nap carpets of cilia still trembled on the innermost reaches of the petals, pointing to the wet warm depths. From the point of view of approaching insects, they shone like the runways at Newark Airport at night, ablaze with seductiveness. It was hoped that the sweet aroma they exuded might go far to suppress the odor of the crimes against nature which had been committed on Garbage Mountain, while their clumped shallow roots might stabilize the surface of the N12.

Maxine had grave doubts about the plan to use inmate labor. She knew that among the prisoners, there would be those who had committed bank robberies, drug-related offenses and nasty white collar larcenies that ruined innocent lives. She really did not want such people messing with her garden. However, when she raised her objections to Sam, who had somehow forged this unique labor agreement, he who almost never smiled could not stop himself from laughing out loud. His contempt told her once again that he and his boss, Jim Brights, believed the Vandeblinken Memorial Garden was memorializing the biggest crook of all, and that the support of BIX was only a way of keeping her, Albert's likely accomplice, in the sights of law enforcement. So she didn't press the matter. She told Mayor Fleeger that she was delighted that so many men from the Correctional Facility had volunteered to help. She promised to endow the decrepit Pettyboro Library with a dozen computers.

The prisoners arrived in buses. They put on their GUMPY gear. They formed a circle around Professor Binkley, who crouched on the ground and demonstrated how the irises must be planted

"The holes should be real shallow," Binkley said, "More like a trench than a hole. The iris rhizome sits sideways in it, like so? See? With the upright sprouting part at the head of the trench, kind of like a woman lying on her side. The long part is the body; the upright part is where she's leaning on her arm." He was thinking of the bronze sculpture of a reclining nude by Henri Matisse, and probably the men from the prison were not, but they had their own memories, and the image worked very well. "You've got to plant the rhizomes four to four and a half inches down, not more. If you go deeper, you might possibly hit plastic diapers."

Maxine moved among the men as they planted the irises. They treated her with respect. They did not look at her twice. She felt no stirring of anyone's loins. She was 67 years old, and it had taken her all the years up to this moment to feel, to *really* feel, that she was over the hill. At first, there on the iris field, it was a bad feeling and depressed her. During the ensuing months, it would gradually become no feeling at all. By the end of that year, it would be an enormous relief.

She had managed to survive the existential threat posed by her beauty. And with any luck, she might still have a few years left in which to enjoy her freedom.

The Pettyboro prisoners came to Garbage Mountain every week-day morning, except for days when the fierce storms with torrential rains returned. Maxine would greet them, standing with Binkley and the Gumrats at the apex of the winding trash dump road, on the threshold of TOXY, waving hello with her gloved hand. She would stay until they were all out planting. Then Marshall would take her off to GUMPY board meetings and fundraising luncheons.

On the last day of the planting, when all the rhizomes were in the ground and the men were ready to depart, Maxine organized a cere-mony of gratitude in their honor. She had received official permission for this event and had insisted that the warden and Mayor Fleeger and Sam, as president of the GUMPY Board, be present, so that it really would be "an event" and help the prisoners feel proud of themselves.

Sam stood with Binkley and Shasta under "Maxie's Rim" and observed Maxine as she made her little speech. He shook his head, muttering about hypocrisy. Shasta shushed him. She wanted to hear what Maxine had to say.

"You have done wonderful work here," she said to the prisoners. "On behalf of the Garbage Mountain Project and the people of New Jersey, I want to thank you for seizing this historic opportunity. I hope that when you next see the garden, it will be green and growing and you will be free men, all debts to society paid off, and you will be able to say to your families, to your children: 'That place there was once a big pile of shit and I helped to disguise it and make it beautiful and put it back into the service of the public.'"

Thereafter, all but 85 of the 4000 irises died in their shallow graves.

The prisoners, hearing of this disaster from a Gumrat who was related to one of them, rooted for the survivors. The image of reclining women persisted in their minds. They counted the days until they would be able to see even a few of their lavender and golden, robins' egg blue and baby pink girls all grown up and blooming.

A SHIPMENT OF HEMLOCKS ARRIVED from Ohio on an FSI flight in early October. To deter potential thieves who might wish to clip one for Christmas, Shasta made sure that "DANGER! PROPERTY OF GUMPY: DELIVER ONLY TO TOXIC GREENHOUSE!" was stenciled in poison green on each canvas-packaged root ball.

At Newark, suspicious USDA inspectors read the frightening root balls (DANGER! TOXIC!) but not the permissions and authorizations that Flora Shipments International had received and filed weeks before, and they quarantined the hemlocks.

Shasta's driver, stuck at the airport since ten in the morning, called at two in the afternoon, helpless and hopelessly frustrated. Shasta drove to Newark with duplicates of all the paperwork. She sent the driver home and took over herself, patiently explaining the situation to the inspectors. They left the airport at the end of their shift, and a new set of inspectors, who had no knowledge of the situation, came on duty, and all the explanations had to begin again. Around midnight, although she didn't want to – *he was such a pisser, so wounded and moody, she was really up to here with him!* – Shasta called Sam.

"Muscle," she pleaded. "Oh please."

The Attorney General of New Jersey called an Under Secretary of Agriculture who called the plant quarantine authorities at Newark International Airport, and by the following midnight, the Ohio hemlocks were being loaded onto Shasta's truck.

She released the passenger seat to maximum and laid her long body down on its side, leaning on her arm, watching Sam. He hung his jacket on a hook in the back, removed his cufflinks and his tie, rolled his sleeves and drove a truck for the first time in 20 years.

It was almost three o'clock on a clear cold autumn night.

Shasta rubbed her cheek against his thigh and kissed the side of his body under his raised driving arm. "Thank you for being so powerful and effective today," she said.

Sam smiled. Breathed. Garbage Mountain disappeared behind them. He pulled her close.

The hemlocks from Ohio died more slowly than the other trees, lasting almost six weeks before withering away. Professor Binkley ordered the GUMRATS to pile the ragged scrap bodies, with their scattered patches of rusted needles, on a flatbed truck and drive them out to a corner of the N12 for burial.

After that, it snowed.

TWENTY-THREE.

First Fruits

A FRUITLESS, HOPELESS WINTER. NOW it was Gumpy's second April. Binkley trudged over his barren spread, wondering if it would be considered chemical warfare and a crime against humanity to load the N12 into canisters and drop it on America's enemies.

He noticed a small black gleam. Thinking it might possibly be a plastic spoon, he went to collect it. He crouched and looked very closely.

It was a sprout.

Binkley stood up, turned his back, walked away. Took a sip of water from his canteen. Closed his eyes tightly. Took another sip of water. Then returned. The sprout was still there. A hemlock. The first newborn vegetation of any kind to lift its head on the N12 since Maxine's training farm had gone into operation.

The young professor forced himself to walk, not sprint, down the slope toward TOXY. "A hemlock," he said breathlessly. "A hemlock seedling." The Gumrats followed him back to the N12 and gathered around the little miracle, reverent as Christmas shepherds. Some of them wept for joy.

Every day, Binkley and his crew went out to observe the sprout. Its greatest advantage was that a certain whitish pestilence, which had been destroying hemlock forests across the mid-Atlantic region, could not survive on Garbage Mountain. So the little tree grew in safety from its chief enemy, slowly but measurably, as though it had no idea it was drinking the dregs of the earth. By the end of the summer, a colony of 36 tiny hemlocks had appeared.

To celebrate Professor Binkley and his amazing N12 hemlock, Maxine decided to have a party. The lavishly decorated invitation called it a "First Fruits" party. In keeping with her Aunt Gladdy's tradition, everybody was invited.

She had already redesigned Albert's Deal Room with just such a happy eventuality in mind. Her contractor had broken through the exterior wall to add a bank of windows. Her decorator had replaced the heavy drapes with diaphanous silks that admitted sunshine and moon glow, had tossed the dark carpet and installed a pale wood floor, stripped the bar and the pool table and stained them white. The walls had been painted the palest possible blue. A white grand piano had been added.

Maxine felt wonderful. She felt that GUMPY had saved her. She was back in control of her life, with nothing to fear. The right ears and eyes were looking in on her. She had no buried treasure to account for and an uncensored guest list.

All the Gumrats came to the party, bringing their dates. Professor Binkley himself brought a voluptuous poetess from Princeton who couldn't keep her hands off him. He was beside himself with happiness. In a few days he would travel west to show off his hemlock to a gathering of some of the most eminent plant scientists in the country. He danced with Maxine and kissed her hand and told her she had changed his life.

State Senator Arroyo arrived with his wife and his entire staff. He had championed GUMPY's funding in the Legislature. He had spearheaded the closing of Garbage Mountain to future dumping, and he had led the fight for reburial and encapsulation of all previous trash. Now he was celebrated as the leading environmental advocate in New Jersey.

What a bash they had that night at Fifteen Willow Cascade! Maxine's caterers set up a steaming Tex-Mex barbecue and a bar in The Moon Garden. A Mexican band wearing huge sombreros jammed on trumpets and strummed guitars. Soon everyone was quaffing margaritas and slurping chili and dancing.

Not Sam. He leaned against the bar, drinking whiskey, watching Shasta dance. He disliked being in Albert's house. He disliked how Shasta looked. Her dress, her bracelets, even her shoes seemed to shoot stars all over like she was trying to be a galaxy. The hands of a hundred men seemed to be reaching for her. He disliked that. Then she waved, her sparkles flying in his direction, and everybody in the place could see that she belonged to him. That helped, but not enough.

"You don't look well," Maxine said, gliding into a spot next to him. "Are you ill?" And to the bartender. "Slivovitz please, Harold."

"Friend of mine died," Sam said. "An Italian cop."

"I'm so sorry to hear that. Was this a young person?"

"Young enough for it to be too soon."

"I hope it was quick and merciful."

"No," he said. "Neither."

"Oh Sam..."

Maxine put her arm around him. She actually put her arm around him. And Sam wanted very much to lay his head down on her shoulder, as he might have done with a real mother, to grieve the loss of his long-time friend and colleague, to comfort himself as he struggled with the realization that it was perfectly possible to die like Vito Branca, with your life's work unfinished, to achieve no justice and make nothing right.

The upsurge of tenderness ended in a flash, each of them feeling that it had been an absurdity.

CEECEE HAD COME TO THE PARTY under duress. Her arthritis was kicking up. She had taken all kinds of pain pills to little effect. Next week the movers were packing her apartment and launching her return to Arizona. Her new house there was being decorated. Her grandkids were at this very moment discussing what kind of cake to bake to welcome her home.

However, her old friend Maxie was taking a different road.

Instead of putting up her feet and relaxing, maybe downsizing sensibly, she had turned into a late-in-life power broker. It looked like the big house would now forever teem with academics and politicians, meetings and parties, and Maxie would just dazzle and hustle and throw her money at bushes and flowers until the end of her days.

Ceecee heard the voice of her tough daughter, Gladdy. *You must know, Mom, that Aunt Maxie is never coming back to Tucson.* She heard her wise daughter, Rosie. *She's not like you, Mom. You hate being a widow, because you loved your husband and wanted him to live forever. She loves being a widow because she was afraid of her husband and wanted him to die so she could play with his money.*

Ceecee sighed. She ate a chicken taco. It was so good that she ate another one. What the hell.

Without warning, Maxine descended like an eagle and dragged her into the center of the festivities. She had the band leader call for silence.

"When we were young, we used to do a number," Maxine said.

"On no, c'mon, no, no, no way..." Ceecee protested, thinking *Please, Maxie. I can't...look at me, for Chrissakes...see how my knees are killing me....*

"I played Ginger Rogers, and Ceecee played Fred Astaire," Maxine continued, "these two ancient performers who were really super famous in those long ago days, and we would dance." Maxine held out her arms. "Fred!"

Everybody was shouting *"go go go go"* and *"Cee-Cee Cee-Cee"* in a rhythmic chorus that would not be denied. Ceecee took Maxine's hand and said, "Okay. Ginger." The band began to play, and the two ladies danced like movie stars, as they had in Sweet Pea, Arizona, when they were girls.

The crowd cheered. *More!* they cried. *More!*

Ceecee's anguished protests finally made it clear to Maxine that there would be no more dancing. So Maxine sat down at the piano and led the crowd in the old songs: *The Four Generals* and *La Paloma* and *Streets of Laredo,* all the old songs from the bygone movies and the forgotten wars and the hard times that, it seemed on this exalted evening, really would come again no more.

Sam settled into the amazingly comfortable brown leather chair that faced the fireplace. A small table beside it held a stack of issues of *Aviation Age*, all dated from the months before Albert had been killed. Sam flipped through them, checking for notations or bent pages, on the chance that Detective Meeker and his crew might have missed some small thing. But they had not.

He began to rummage among the photos in the Vandeblinken family albums. Brand new albums, he noted. Displayed on the coffee table, inviting all onlookers, as obvious as an infomercial. Hadn't there been some photos of his dad from years back? He wondered if his mother had them in an album. He came across several pictures of Frank Dash as he rode through Central Park in his go-cart with his dogs and his tripods, a determined little man necklaced with light meters and lenses.

"He was a genius," Ceecee said, flopping down on the flowered chair adjacent to the brown leather, pulling off her shoes, rubbing her knees and her swollen ankles.

"So I've been told. How did she meet him?"

"He came into the showroom with one of his models to buy some dresses. Me and Maxie, we lived there. It was a barter deal. Maxie's Uncle Harry's boss gave us two beds in the back, head to head, with a lamp between. In exchange, we worked there after school, me sewing, Maxie modeling. Frank Dash saw Maxie and boom, right away he wanted her."

Ceecee took a joint from her beaded purse and lit up. Sam declined her offer to share.

"He brought us to his studio. In the wardrobes, Frank had all these costumes. Maxie would put them on, and I would make them fit her perfect, never too tight, just right. We dressed her up like Diana and Athena and Tosca and Juliet, and Frank would take pictures. Every time she put on a costume, Maxie felt a little better about being beautiful. Which was good because up to that time, before Frank, she felt really bad about it. Things got very screwed up because Maxie was so beautiful.

"One of my teachers in Frank's studio was the most important Victorian bustle maker in the costume business at that time. He taught me how to control fabric. And a master boot maker named Crispin, oh, he was something wonderful, he taught me everything else. Soon I felt like I was skilled enough to leave Maxie and still be okay." Ceecee took a long drag and grinned contentedly. "So I went out to LA where my mother lived and I got myself a pretty big career."

Shasta swept into the living room, sparkling with a story she wanted to tell Sam. He gave her a fierce look and said "Not now." She backed out of the room.

"Wow. She's scared of you. Our big tough Shasta!" Ceecee turned to get a better look at him. "Do you enjoy that, Mr. Euphemia? Does that turn you on? Are you like Albert?"

He leaned forward suddenly, so forcefully that the chair tipped.

"How scared did Albert make Maxine?" he asked. "Did he threaten her?"

"Oh fuck I shouldn't have said that, it was just a smartass remark and I'm not saying another word."

He loomed over her, insistent, his eyebrows hunched together. He was biting his words like he was trying not to eat her, clenching his fists like he was trying not to seize her. Ceecee wanted to flee, as Shasta had fled. But her damn knees would not allow that.

"Did he threaten her? Was he violent?"

"Never, he never... Leave me alone."

"Was he a vengeful guy? Like if somebody pissed him off, or crossed him, or hurt him in some way, did he go after them?" Sam couldn't help himself, he grabbed her hands. "Please. Just tell me this. If Albert had known who murdered his son, would he have gone looking for vengeance?"

"Let go!"

"C'mon, Mrs. Blochner, please."

"Let go!"

"You spent time with him. Real quality like social time. C'mon, venture a guess." He gave up her hands because he saw that she was alarmed, and he so didn't want that. "Please. Tell me. How scary was Albert? If he could, I mean if he could write it into his will, send a posthumous directive, if he could rise from the dead and arrange it, would he have done anything, whatever it took, anything to track down his son's killers?"

Trapped in Maxie's chair, facing a desperate man who was, Ceecee knew, only really seeking the truth, she relented. "He might have," she said, imagining the daggers of the Turks. "Possibly."

part

———————

8

TWENTY-FOUR.

Advice for the Bride-to-Be

Aunt Gladdy had begged her not to marry Frank. "You're 19 years old. He's past 40."

"I love him."

"It's not suitable."

"I really love him, Aunt Gladdy. He is wonderful. I feel wonderful when I am with him. And anyway, since when did suitability mean anything to you?"

"You're normal size. He's a dwarf."

"He loves me."

"Of course, he loves you! Why wouldn't a lonely midget photographer love his most beautiful model? And if he loves you so much why tell me why does he want you to pose naked? Is that what a man in love does with his bride-to-be? Shows her body to the whole world? He's exploiting you."

Maxine laughed. "Oh sweet Aunt Gladdy, you're such a dumb utopian, you never see the truth about people. I've got nothing. Frank is successful and rich and ready to move me into a big apartment on Central Park West. I'm an uneducated twerp. He's brilliant and talented and ready to transform me into an educated, cultured person. Seems to me, if anybody's being exploited, it's Frank. By me."

"Maxie, please, listen to me. If you are drawn to this man, then be with him, be his lover if you must although I can't see how you could find such a grotesque fellow attractive, but please please I beg you don't take him as a husband. Marriage is a finality, a commitment, a promise! For God's sake don't promise yourself to Frank Dash!"

"I am going to marry him, Aunt Gladdy. My mind is set."

"He's like Richard the Third! A deformed sorcerer who has somehow cast his spell over you!"

"He is a great artist. And stop calling him a dwarf and a midget and grotesque and deformed! He's the nicest person I have ever known! You're supposed to be a liberal. Get over how he looks."

Gladdy sniffed and turned aside. Maxine's words had stung her pride. She was indeed ashamed to have been so bigoted toward an afflicted soul. But that was as far as it went.

Maxine was saying "I want you to give me away at the wedding."

"I will not even come to your wedding, that's how strongly I feel about this. In fact, I won't even be here. I'll be on a boat heading for the holy land."

"Change your ticket. Get the next boat. If it's a matter of money, Frank will help."

"I would never take money from that bastard."

Maxine sighed. "I'm beginning to give up on you, Aunt Gladdy."

"Oh, how I wish Ceecee were here! She would be practical and smart. She would convince you."

"Ceecee is in Hollywood working on a movie and dating a gigantic dolly grip and taking night school classes in business. Every minute of her day is spoken for. But when I asked her to come back to New York and stand up for me at my wedding, she said sure, absolutely. She didn't say sorry, I have to be on a fucking *boat!*"

"This is a dangerous marriage for you, Maxie!"

"Dangerous?! Listen to Aunt Clueless, going off to pick peaches under the bombs of the Syrians."

"He's a dwarf! That is from birth! It's in the blood! What if you get pregnant?!"

"I am pregnant."

Gladys Klein literally tore her hair. "Are you crazy?! What if the baby turns out like Frank?!"

"That's the idea, you stupid bitch!"

Gladys slapped her. Maxine did not cry. But Gladys did.

"I gave you a good doctrine," she wept. "And you have forsaken it in order to have a ridiculous life without wisdom or purpose with a man who uses you like a piece of garbage."

In the end, it was her Uncle Harry who walked Maxine across Frank's living room at the little wedding, into Frank's arms, into his life and his astonishing legacy. It was Rosita who made the towering wedding cake, which, the groom quipped, was almost as big as he was. Uncle Harry's boss brought the champagne, as a tribute to the days when Maxine modeled swimsuits for him. And behind her, carrying her flowers, bearing her ring, wearing lilac lace and the first pair of boots she had ever personally made, was Gladys Klein's little Aztec queen, Celestita Rodriguez.

TWENTY-FIVE.
Ceecee

CEECEE WAS TOO TIRED TO go home after the party. She took some pills for her aches and pains and stayed in one of the guest bedrooms and woke up with different aches and pains in the morning. Limping to the window, she watched Maxine sprawled on her chaise under the dogwoods, sucking on one of her lemons, cracking ice with her back teeth like a puppy, and already on the phone doing business. She seemed like a total stranger to Ceecee this morning. In fact, she had seemed that way for quite some time.

She walked slowly down the stairs, her knees speaking up at every step. At the bottom, the ever-thoughtful Muir handed her a cup of coffee. The sight of the Baluchistan carpets in the living room put a smile on her face and banished her discomforts.

Of all the glorious objects in Maxie's house, Ceecee loved those carpets most. She imagined the weavers with their veils and their nimble fingers, gossiping as they tied the million tiny knots of the inspired pattern. Praise, oh sing praise for the peace of making things! No business no money no pressure just the rapture of working and working until the new beauty entered the world, and the world was changed. Ceecee thought that when she finally got home to her desert, she would study the knots and consider weaving.

But in Maxie's house, the phone was ringing. Important conversations were developing. The cleaning crew had just arrived, preparing to launch the roar of their machines.

Ceecee took her coffee outside. Perfect weather, for once. She waited for Maxine to get off the phone. "You need to stop taking calls now and get dressed and take this old lady home," she said.

Maxine rose up and hugged her. Soon they were on their way to New York, gossiping about the party guests. Ceecee did not tell Maxine about her conversation with Sam. Why ruin a great morning?

HER FIRST THOUGHT WHEN SHE FOUND her apartment door ajar was Alzheimer's. She had left her place unlocked overnight in New York City. A sure sign of mental dissolution. The end had come.

However, when she and Maxine entered the apartment and Crispy ran to them, his perky whiskers smeared with cheese and his breath reeking, Ceecee saw the truth. Someone had broken in, neutralized her dog with tasty treats, and ransacked her home.

The sofas had been torn apart, their pillows tumbled. The dining room chairs were lying on their arms and backs. The papers and designs in Ceecee's studio office were scattered, every folder opened, the colors smeared, the tissue torn, the leather samples thrown all over and the drafting table flipped on its face. The bathroom cabinet poured pills into the sink. In the bedrooms, quilts had been dragged from their mattresses. Open drawers spilled sweaters, nightgowns, jewelry. Every closet had been searched, the coats and dresses crushed on the floor. Ceecee gagged, sickened when she saw that the spare underwear and socks of her granddaughters had been handled. She clutched her head, feeling the smash of the dirt road.

In the cabinet within the closet hidden within the short hall to the kitchen, the complex codes that opened the gun cabinet had been breached. The deadly weapon lay casually on the counter like a cook book. *And absolutely nothing was missing!*

Ceecee staggered from the kitchen, her heart racing. She needed help! She needed Maxie!

She needed her Gladdy, her Rosie, she needed PuPu and Herman, she needed Lila with her hatchet, Maxie with her knife!

Where was Maxie?!

She found Maxine circling the apartment, room after room, around and around, breathing hard, making a deep-throated growling noise. Ceecee realized that her poor old friend had been overthrown by panic and could not help her.

She rang the doorman and told him to call the cops.

Maxine leaped, wrenching the phone away. "No no call him back tell him not to call the cops! Don't you realize the cops can be bought! Albert bought cops all the time!"

"Shhh stop take it easy," Ceecee said. "I need to think. I need to be calm."

"No listen to me listen..."

"Stop. You're getting crazy."

And Maxine did look crazy to Ceecee at that moment. Her eyes were wild. Her hair was flying. "It could be his enemies," she was whispering. "It could be his friends. They want to know what I'm saying. They're afraid I'm going to tell you something. Don't you see? They broke in so they could bug the place! The place is bugged now! Don't you understand, that's what they do! They put listening devices all over..."

"Stop."

"They're sending a message. Oh God. They're saying we won't hurt you now but any time we want to, we can hurt you, we can get to anyone..."

"I said STOP!" Ceecee shouted. "This is my house! This is my stuff all over the floor and my kids' pictures all smashed up, and I don't need a bunch of paranoid shit from you at this moment!"

"But I'm right! I know! Listen to me! Oh God how can you not understand that they hear everything?! How can you be such a fool?!"

Ceecee shoved her against a wall, angry beyond control.

"Don't call me a fool! You're the one who bedded down with terrible guys. You're the one who looked for trouble and fucked it and made it part of your life, and that's your craziness, all yours, it has nothing to do with me and my family and you're the one who is a fool and...and... and just get the hell away from me!"

"Stop talking! They're listening! I'll show you I'll show you I'll show you what they do!"

Maxine raced into the bathroom, clamored into the shower stall and began feeling the tiles, looking for loose ones. Ceecee watched her, wracked with pity to see her friend reduced to such madness in her old age.

"The police will be here in a couple of minutes," Ceecee said. "If you want them to find you standing in the shower feeling up the soap dish, stay where you are. Otherwise get out of my house."

"Ceecee, listen to me!"

"Go, dammit! Get yourself gone! Get out."

Back in her own house, Maxine chewed a piece of lemon peel like a rabbit, with her front teeth. When the peel was gone, she kept on chewing. Click, click, click, went her teeth, the unconscious chatter of a mind gone wild with fear.

Why would they suddenly attack Ceecee? Surely, it was to show Maxine that they were still watching her, that nobody she loved was safe. She must have caught their attention by selling the contents of Albert's vault for charitable causes, oh God she must have made them nervous by letting Detective Meeker re-bug the house and allowing BIX to dominate the GUMPY Board.

Didn't they understand that the only way to handle these snoopers was to embed them in her affairs, so that they could never see clearly because they could never see from a distance?

Didn't the widely feared Sam Euphemia hound her with his gruesome accident reports, didn't he ask her repeatedly for a list of dinner guests? Surely these Albertine spies, who could slither into Ceecee's house like midnight roaches, must be aware that she had never told him anything Somehow, she had to reassure them or the next attack might be worse. They might go after the children. They might infest the Silver Smith studios and go after Lila's grandkids, or Paul and Brigitte in Hong Kong or the sweet Gumrats. No one would be safe, and everyone would blame her and despise her as Ceecee did now, her rock, her sister since forever, her defender who had saved her from the hellish basement – oh God, what a look of pity and disgust had crossed her face! – and all Maxine's attempts to live not like a whore but like a decent woman with a family and colleagues and a meritorious purpose would be blasted away and she would have no one, no one, no one in the whole world.

TWENTY-SIX.

L'Arena

MAXINE CHECKED INTO THE SAME hotel in Verona where Albert had imprisoned her so many years before. She did everything possible to be noticed. She told the desk clerk and the concierge that she was going to the opera at L'Arena. She made sure that she mentioned that she was sitting in the lower tier and even specified the seat number. She wore her eye-catching pink vintage Chanel suit. She believed that every nook and byway of the ancient market town must be inlaid with Albert's associates and that they would seize her at any moment.

During their marriage, Maxine and Albert had regularly attended L'Arena performances. They were listed as patrons of the company and wined and dined for their generosity. Although she had not been in town since his death, she was instantly recognized by one of the house managers. He came rushing up the stone steps to her side to explain how much her dear husband was missed. What a tragedy, what a loss! She smiled at him and thanked him for his concern. She figured this was it.

The house manager alerted the development director to her presence. Soon the hungry fundraiser was kissing her hand, telling her how beautiful she looked, what a delight and an honor to have her back in Verona. Why had she not called? He would have made arrangements! Would she not join him and the opera's stars for a private dinner after the performance? Maxine gladly accepted. The fundraiser departed. Maxine tracked him with her opera glasses, convinced that every usher and security man he spoke to was really there not to usher or provide security but to watch her, that they all somehow worked for Albert's successors. Ready for abduction, she endured the trumpets and the elephants.

At the interact, she loudly asked an usher the location of the ladies' room, even though she knew perfectly well where it was. During the curtain calls, she asked another usher how to reach the stage door, even though she had been backstage many times. Despite these dropped crumbs, no one seemed to be following her.

When the performance ended, an entourage of sycophants led her into the Plaza. Great crowds swirled around them. The cafes overflowed with music lovers, and the din of their conversations in a dozen languages, their laughter and singing filled the night.

Maxine felt suddenly very tired. She knew she could not sit through a dinner party now. She begged her companions to understand. They nodded sympathetically. An old lady, after all; bereaved. She waited alone for a moment while someone went to find her a cab. And a metal hook closed around her arm.

THE WOMAN'S EYES WERE HARD TO SEE, buried as they were in dark pouches and shadows. Her skin was gray. Her hair was gray, only a little of the original black remaining. She was an old woman with the stride and strength of someone still young. Maxine had never dreamed she would be alive, that the butchers would have lopped a hand from a breathing body.

The woman steered Maxine into the back of a car where Maxine's bag had already been stowed. The car began to move. Maxine cleared her throat and summoned the low steady power voice of a scientist she had once played in an industrial for pesticides.

"Now listen, please. You must listen to me," she said. "I have come to Verona specifically to reassure you that I am no danger to you. I know nothing about your business. I knew nothing about it when Albert was alive. My friends and my family, they know nothing, I have never told them anything that would harm you because I do not know anything that would harm you. Please. You must believe that and leave them alone. You must not frighten them or invade their lives. They know nothing. I have been questioned and hounded by all kinds of authorities for years, and I have never told them anything because I have nothing to tell them. I know nothing about your business. I do not even know who you are."

"I am Francesca," the woman said. "I worked for Inspector Vito Branca who died last week after a terrible long illness."

They crossed the silent Adige and traversed the avenues around the Museum, then doubled back toward the house that, tourists were told, belonged to Romeo's innocent bride, Juliet, and then finally sped onto the Milan highway. All the while, Francesca talked. When Maxine began to sag from exhaustion, the powerful hook held her upright.

"At Inspector Branca's office, we are working on the file we call 'Plane Crashes. Not Explained.' Very frustrating. Dead ends and mysteries. Then we have a big break. Your husband contacts us. He is full of grief and anger because his son has been murdered in Zurich. You remember this time, Signora?"

"Yes."

"Albert has decided to give us a list of all his old customers and trading partners from the days when he was still making Sofias. Because he is sure one of them is responsible for the death of his son. We are excited. We think the list will lead us to the killer planes, and we will be able to bring them down from the sky.

"We must find a way to protect your Albert, to make sure no one knows he has contacted the police. So I go to meet him in Monaco. I dress up myself and pretend to be one of those women who try to get on with wealthy men. I expect to return home with the list. But when I wake up I have no list and no left hand. In the hospital, my colleagues tell me that Albert is dead. They have his blood and his clothing and pictures of his body – but no body. We think the people on his list, the people who killed the son, they have learned Albert has gone to Inspector

Branca and they have now ordered the execution of the father. We think that for a long time. We follow all the leads.

"They do not prove out.

"Then we begin to think like Detective Meeker from New Jersey that you are the one who has had Albert killed. We read everything Sam Euphemia has to say about you and your life and your friends." With her haunted eyes, she searched Maxine's face. "Meeker's idea does not prove out either. Sam tells us that you are much too cynical and greedy to care about some affair that Albert might be having, that all you desire is his money and you are quite content that he is dead.

"We are at a loss."

Maxine closed her eyes. She wanted so badly just to sleep.

"But then, just the other day, Sam reports that your friend says 'Possibly.'"

Maxine squinted at Francesca in the dark car. What was she talking about?

"Sam asks your friend...Cecilia..."

"Celestita. Ceecee."

"Sam asks her: if Albert could rise from the dead, would he seek revenge for his son's death? And she says 'Possibly.' One word. This one word makes us think seriously about an idea Sam has had for some time.

"We begin to think that my left hand has been used to make everyone believe Albert is killed by a jealous lover, and that those pictures of him lying in all that blood are just like the Sofias, very clever deceptions, which allow him to live on in secret and be free to hunt for the murderers of his son.

"What do you think, Signora? Is this something your Albert might do?"

Maxine closed her eyes. Without realizing it, she had begun to beat her fist gently against her heart.

"I tell to Sam that you say so little because you must be very afraid," Francesca said. "Who would not be afraid of such a demon husband? But now that you have come here like this, in your pink suit, to confront the monsters in person, I will tell to Sam and Mr. Brights and Meeker and all our people, this is a strong woman, and in her way, very brave."

MAXINE HAD EXPECTED TO SUMMON a faceless taxi when she crossed back into America. Instead she saw Sam. He called her name and strode toward her, his brow furrowed with concern and urgent sympathy. She had never seen that expression on his face before.

She felt so cold suddenly, as though the blood in her veins had stopped flowing and had just frozen in place. Her feet were so cold she couldn't stand on them. She staggered. Her knees buckled. Sam caught her before she fell.

"Something has happened...what has happened?!" she cried. It was Ceecee flying out to her new house! It was Professor Binkley flying west to show off his hemlock! It was one of Shasta's couriers oh my God it was Shasta! "Don't try to lie to me, I know you now, I can read your face. *Who has fallen out of the sky?!*

"No worries. Everything's okay. Everyone is safe. I talked to Francesca."

HE DROVE HER TO A CERTAIN POINT on the Turnpike, a particular junction of vast space and sky and motion between the airport and the port. It was past two in the morning but there was still quite a bit of traffic, traveling fast. If the sky had stars, they were made invisible by the glare of commerce from below.

Sam pulled over into the breakdown lane and put on his flashers and stopped. "I want to show you something," he said.

He got out of the car and circled around behind it and opened Maxine's door, unlocked her seat belt and lifted her out.

"What what leave me what is this? Stop!" she shouted, beating at him as, dodging the sporadic traffic, he ran with her across the highway. Her shoes fell off. Someone's wheels crushed them. He set her down on the concrete barrier and climbed up next to her and pulled her upright.

Maxine was shrieking. The traffic blurred, roaring. She couldn't hear her own cries. Icy winds tore apart her hair and billowed back her jacket. Her nose poured. An 18-wheeler thundered past. She saw herself smashed like the shoes. But Sam had locked her in place with iron hands, holding her more tightly than she had ever been held before.

"Look around," he yelled. "Right here. This is the place. The best place. I loved this place when I was a kid. I used to ride my bike out to the Turnpike and stand here, right here until the cops pulled me off." He laughed and turned her so she could see in every direction. "Look. Look around. Stop screaming, it's okay it's okay. I've got you. Open your eyes. You got four lanes of traffic going north to New York. And four lanes of traffic going south to Delaware. And you got the port of Newark to the east, see? With the big container ships and the cargo hanging in the air, ready to go go go. On the west you got the airport. Millions of people. Millions of tons of cargo. The whole world arriving and leaving. Now look up...look at the planes, lined up in the sky. See the lights? You can see four sets of lights from incoming aircraft. You know there's hundreds more right behind them. If you turn around, come on, turn around, you're okay, I've got you, you see hundreds more on their way out. It's a couple hours before dawn, and everything is here and moving. The money and the machines and the trees and the art and the garbage, the whole world's business and travel and plans for the future! It's all right here! And you think, Jesus, how great is this, to be able to be here now in this time, to be this free, to be able to move move move, *any time*, *everywhere*, send, receive, escape, escape from everything! Who's been able to do that, Maxine? We're the first! We're the wind!"

Maxine began to cry.

Horrors unburied poured from her eyes. Her Uncle Harry was blubbering and sputtering. A terrible accident. She was beating on his belly to keep him from saying another word. The ropes were cutting her. The whores were laughing. The cowboy was holding his skinny penis in his hand, tapping her with it, touching her mouth, her breasts. She was down on the floor of the train bathroom, scratching up the sticky bills while the soldier called her a stupid cunt. And when she looked up, she saw her baby boy, stillborn, all gray; she saw her darling Frank, tumbled off his chair in his dark room, the beautiful pictures bathing in shallow tubs all around him and his great heart stopped. Every tear she had not shed in all the years fell onto the New Jersey Turnpike.

Sam put her back in his car and drove her home and did not leave her until she was sedated and sleeping in her bed and armed guards were stationed around her house and he could be absolutely sure that she was okay.

MAXINE THOUGHT OF THE EYES that watched her, the machines that listened to her in these years since Albert's departure. She had done everything possible to reduce the scrutiny, but it had just metastasized. It didn't matter what her reasons were, whether she loved Albert truly or stayed loyal to him out of fear or whether she just wanted to inherit his loot, it didn't matter. She had caused the sky to rain death. Her loyalty was a side effect of her greed, and her greed was a crime against nature, and her silence, her willful, terror-stricken silence, the true disaster.

"You don't deliberately go out to meet complicity and embrace it," she wrote to Sam, copies to Meeker and Francesca. "You step into it, like a puddle, by not paying attention, because you are so self-absorbed. You say this is my life, there's been enough mess in it already, I'm entitled to some peace and comfort now, and that mess over there is not part of my life. You say this at the very same time that you are walking through the mess because of course, it is not over there, it is underfoot, under your pillow, under your fingernails. Dig and you will see it. But you don't want to dig. You want to live well and sleep tight and make sure that the people you care about have enough money to keep clear of the mess. I thought if I did what my Aunt Gladdy said – planted the earth and shared the bounty – I would have a handle on rightness. But planting happens only in the top layer, isn't that right? If you dig down deeper, you hit all the evil stuff that will never degrade or go away.

"The people on the enclosed list may have played pool with my husband after I was sent to bed. They may have written him letters, never emails, they never did emails, letters which he later burned, or left him messages on the machine, which I may have heard by chance, which he later erased. I knew these people only on a first-name basis, and the names I was given may have been false, so in addition to my memories of the letters and the phone messages, I am also sending you physical descriptions, of which I am more sure, in case those can prove helpful. Whatever else I chanced to know, all of which is included here, usually came from snippets of small talk: a company name, a favorite vacation spot, complaints about an ex-wife's extravagance, a child's addiction, a food allergy or a preference for a certain kind of vodka. Occasionally I admired a beautiful car in the driveway and saw its license plate, despite wanting not to, without really meaning to, by chance, by glance. So that is here as well. Sometimes these things stick in one's mind. I was always a quick study, learned lines in a flash for every role I was asked to play.

"What exact connection these people may have had to my husband's business I cannot say because, as you know, I am only an entertainer, a party-thrower, decorator of barren spaces. I have lived my life in the top layer, the clean new soil that costs so fucking much, the pretty part."

TWENTY-SEVEN.
The Calder

SHE WOULD NOT SELL THE house and leave, nor would she allow anyone to move in with her.

She sent Muir into an affluent retirement, both of them weeping at their goodbyes.

Jim Brights, whom she had never actually met, showed up at her beauty salon, sitting in a pink plastic chair in his raincoat and waiting among the fashion magazines like some docile husband for her to be finished with her manicure so he could take her out for coffee and talk to her. He turned out to be an old bald guy leaning on a cane, his face a lively mask of wrinkles that looked very much like a route map. His chauffeur-driven Chevy cruised along behind them as he walked her down the wet street.

"I have to stay," she told him. "I have to be alone. What if he comes for me? I must be alone when he comes."

Jim kissed her hand. He loaded her house and her cars with a level of security never dreamed of by Detective Meeker.

From the Gumrats, she accepted a labradoodle named Julie as a companion for darling old Hannibal, much slowed down by years and now losing his sight. However, the strong young bitch was too frolicsome for Hannibal to keep up with, and her usefulness as a watchdog was limited by her sweet temper and the fact that she slept so soundly.

Maxine started getting rid of her remaining possessions.

She gave the Borgia lanterns to UNJPB for its new nanotechnology institute, with a note that said "If you'd rather have money than these relics, go ahead, sell them, I will not be in the least offended."

She arrived at the party to launch Arroyo's campaign for Congress with a jacket of soft gray Mongolian leather to replace the jacket which had been ruined on Garbage Mountain years before. It was too big, but she figured he would find it worth altering.

Whenever one of the Gumrats received a PhD or got married, Maxine bestowed some chunk of her stash: a pair of sterling silver Tiffany candlesticks, still in their light blue box; the scarlet Zapata; a Rookwood vase.

Ivan Binkley was hired away from PB by the University of California at Davis, his future further guaranteed because he shared in the patent of the N12 hemlocks. Stunted versions of their Ohio Christmas tree ancestors, they had shallow, wide-ranging roots and an unprecedented resistance to certain usually lethal chemical compounds. When Binkley walked off the plane in Sacramento, carrying the seedlings like an EMT carrying a life-saving organ, he was greeted by great scholars, all begging him for the whole story. He told them everything and went into some detail about the eccentric, rich old lady who had invented the idea of the N12 training farm and encouraged GUMPY's research through trials and failures and had thrown such a whopping big bash when they succeeded. Not just a patroness, he told the professors. More like a fairy godmother.

Maxine gave him the ebony bookcases for his new office.

She engraved affectionate messages on the inside of her two remaining gold bangles and gave them to Shasta, who wore them frequently, and always when flying, one on each wrist, like Wonder Woman.

To Ceecee, as a house warming gift, she sent the Baluchistan carpets.

"Come to us here," Ceecee wrote. "Stop all this foolishness and be old already and come home."

"Soon," Maxine responded. "Soon. I promise. As soon as possible. It's just not possible yet."

She gave Sam Euphemia the brown leather chair, as well as a framed copy of the legislation that changed the name of the earth works on Garbage Mountain to "The Pettyboro Memorial Garden", in honor of the men who had died there so long ago.

The long fox cape hung in her closet, splendid, politically incorrect, un-givable. She was just stuck with it. Sometimes, she slept under it and dreamed of Albert.

Fifteen Willow Cascade grew lighter, dustier, worn. Still, Maxine would not move. She waited, keeping herself so busy with GUMPY affairs that she almost forgot that really she was waiting for Albert to return and punish her for an act of disloyalty that had led to the recovery of many precious stolen art works, the exposure of warehouses filled with bogus aircraft parts, the arrest of their owners, distributors and customers and the grounding of countless airplanes around the world.

THE PERFUME OF THE MOCK ORANGE greeted him.

He stopped for a moment and inhaled.

With the tips of his gloved fingers, he touched the startling white faces of the zinnias. He noted with pleasure the bench he had sent from England; then realized it was rather weather-beaten. Why didn't she have it refinished?

The pale roses, which had grown as high as the house, stirred above him, whispering welcome home. He looked up, expecting to see the Borgia palace lanterns which he had missed at the front gate. But they were not here. And where was the birdbath? Had she sold these things? No, she loved them too much; could not have parted with them; must have relocated them in some other corner of the garden. He looked around. But where?

He entered the house easily for she had not changed the locks. Noted the new refrigerator. Drifted into the Deal Room on silent feet and gasped. She had changed everything! Painted it all an insipid blue, the color of a Watteau sky. Where were the portraits of his champion greyhounds? Who was that curly haired dog snoring under the...the... *was that white thing his billiard table?!* She had even acquired a white piano! *Mein Gott, Maxie, was Liberace coming to dinner?!*

When he entered the living room and saw that his Rookwood vases were gone, his gorgeous rugs so laboriously bargained for, and that his chair, *his chair,* his wonderful brown leather chair had disappeared, he became enraged. The one thing of his that was still in its place was the silly Calder mobile. Fuming, he reached up and batted it, making it whirl and tilt. Then he took a moment to calm himself, fearing to set off another heart attack.

Bad enough that she had betrayed him. But in addition, she had erased him from his own home. Obliterated his possessions, his passions, his treasures! What madness had caused him ever to dote so upon the irrational American witch?

He walked up the stairs to the bedroom. She was sleeping in one of his old silk shirts, next to pictures of him and Hannibal that grinned at her from the bedside table. In a flash, his anger disappeared. His heart melted. He sat down on the bed next to her. "How I missed you, my darling girl," he whispered, stroking her hair, touching her shoulder with his lips.

Maxine opened her eyes and frowned. She saw before her a man about 50 years old, in a black leather coat. He had black hair and no beard. "What have you done to yourself? What happened to your beard? You were so attractive…"

"Ah, well. So now I am *young* and attractive," he joked.

His flecked hazel eyes had turned brown, all crow's feet and dark pouches eradicated. His bushy brows were now thin. They slanted downward toward his ears, giving him a sad, gentle aspect. His thin lips had been made full, his long, crooked nose reduced in size and straightened. *His dimples were gone!* And his teeth had changed. His beautiful smile that lit her mornings was now filled with yellow teeth. The final irony for her Albert, to be disguised as a smoker.

"I liked you better my way," Maxine murmured.

Albert trailed his fingers down the front of her body, leaving a warm path of memories on the silk shirt. Maybe she was dreaming, she thought. Then she thought no.

"It was necessary," he said. "My boy's death had to be avenged. There had to be justice. For that, I needed to be hidden."

He pulled her up into his arms and kissed her and hugged her, and she pressed her mouth against his ear, tasting the scars that pulled the veil so tightly over his former face.

It was wonderful for them both, to hold each other again.

It was just wonderful.

They almost could not let go.

"You had everything you wanted," he said. "And now you have... what? Sold it?"

"Sold it, some. Given it away."

He settled onto his back next to her. She rested her head on his shoulder. He embraced her with his right arm. She sighed with pleasure at the familiar brand of his cold watch on her back.

"And why did you keep the Calder? Why that one thing?"

"Oh, it was just because of a memory. Mr. Calder's assistant came to our apartment to pick up Frank's photographs of his sculptures. I tried to behave like a grown-up and served iced tea and cheese and crackers. Frank told me that the sculptures represented Mr. Calder's understanding of force and motion and freedom. And I knew when I married you and took everything you had to offer, I would lose all that. So I kept the Calder to remind me."

Maxine reached up with both arms from the bed and the man and her fate and stretched as far as she could. "I would have gotten rid of it, Albert, just like everything else. But nobody wanted it. It's a fake. Somebody fooled you."

"You fooled me. I never thought you would. Why were you not loyal to me, Maxie?"

"You attacked my friend. My sister."

"Not to hurt her. Only to keep you afraid of me."

"I could bear that you were a thief but not that you were a murderer." She sat up, twisted and turned to get a good look at him. "Was it worth it? Did you find the people who killed Marcus?"

He would not answer her. And even if he had, she would not have known if he told the truth, so deep was his cover, so expressionless had his disguise left his face.

"You gave away my chair," he said.

"You took away my freedom," she responded.

"And did you love your freedom more than you loved me?"

"Yes."

He might have plunged his knife into her heart then or smothered her with one of the pillows, or maybe he would have rolled toward her and just slept in her arms, a sick, tired old man, ready to rest. But his half-blind comrade, Hannibal, awakened by the sound of his voice and the unforgotten smell of him, came running across the hallway and onto the bed, barking with joy and licking him and hugging him with his soft paws.

Albert embraced his dog and kissed his wife, for they were the only creatures left alive in this world who still knew, really knew, who he was, and then he left.

Hannibal whimpered and whined. Maxine held him, whispering: "Shhh my poor dear, it's not what you think. It was just a terrible criminal who disguised himself as the one we love. Hush now, shhhh, shhhh, shhhh."

Of course, there were pictures and recordings of Albert's visit. His new face and body would be broadcast to all those who so tirelessly sought for the guilty to hang for their crimes. How could Maxine explain to them that Albert had in fact already been caught, his child and all his life's work destroyed, his treasure scattered, and he himself buried alive inside his own body, a walking grave?

How could she explain that it was she who had escaped punishment, who had been saved from retribution by the merest scent of true love?

As the vast excavations little by little swallowed the old landfill, Garbage Mountain began to melt and reform itself into a ridge of dun-colored earthworks outlying the Turnpike. Intermittently, curled gas pipes protruded, a stalagmite flock, grazing on fields of dirt, waiting to be milked of ether. Enterprising individuals who tried to sneak up in the darkness to drop their rusted car parts or construction rubble or outdated computer components were fined heavily when the Troopers caught them and given stern lectures on environmental protection.

The only sector of the old Garbage Mountain that remained uncapped was the N12, where Binkley and the Gumrats had roamed and so many varieties of flora had been tried and tested and found dead. Thinly coated by whatever gravel the wind and the rain provided, the N12 now wore random grasses, scattered clumps of varicolored iris, and a small grove of hemlocks.

A landscape architect, who had won a statewide competition with her design, set to work planting the remaining 68 acres with grass. She managed occasional beds of bayberry and holly and all the sumacs, easy-going local road-siders, to accompany the paths that crisscrossed the new hills. She secured the paths with creeping thyme, so that visitors would raise a lovely pungent smell underfoot with every step. As the plantings took hold, drivers on the Turnpike noticed a green sheen on what had once been Garbage Mountain. Many assumed it was chemical slime leaking to the surface. However, it was explained in full-page ads in the local newspapers and in a dozen political campaigns, with every politician taking credit, that the green was a budding, soon to grow into a magnificent park. So successful was the new project that efforts had begun to halt further development on a couple of thousand acres surrounding it, to create there a network of tidal ponds, a nature preserve and a refuge for the besieged wildlife of the Garden State.

THE PETTYBORO MEMORIAL GARDEN EVENTUALLY opened to the public. It had a resident naturalist and volunteer docents and picnic tables. It had a museum lodged in TOXY, where students of adaptation and concealment could come and study the annals of the Gumrats. In this museum, there were also tall, see-through sarcophagi of glass that contained borings from the original Garbage Mountain – cross sections of the earth, with its history exposed, the azure rocks and detergent bottles, obsolete gadgets and clothes and toys, all the stuff once wanted so passionately, purchased so dearly, so the people could contemplate the mistakes of the past and everything that had been buried and disguised and almost forgotten.

Pictures of the long dead men memorialized by the Garden were dug out of family albums and mounted permanently in display cases. These included pictures of Angelo Euphemia, standing with his brother Joe and their mother, on a sunny dirt road near a church in Sicily; laughing at his wedding with his pretty American wife; posing with his crew on the big pipes they were about to lay into the earth; holding his little boy in his strong arms.

Becket, May 2018

Acknowledgments

I am grateful to those dear critics who have read
this book through many drafts: Suzanne Braun Levine,
Julie Brickman, Martha Ronk and Jenny Stodolsky.

Other Books by Susan Dworkin

Making Tootsie
Stolen Goods
The Commons
The Ms. Guide to a Woman's Health (with Dr. Cynthia W. Cooke)
The Nazi Officer's Wife (with Edith Hahn Beer)
The Book of Candy
The Viking in the Wheat Field
Weeding Out the Tears (with Jeanne White)
Desperately Seeking Susan (novelization of the film)
Miss America 1945

To find out more about this author, go to her website:
www.susandworkin.com

Or send a message to
dividedlightprojects@gmail.com

Made in the USA
Middletown, DE
05 March 2019